The TRaiN of DaRK WoNDERS

ALex BeLL

ROCK THE BOAT

A Rock the Boat Book

First published in Great Britain, the Republic of
Ireland and Australia by Rock the Boat,
an imprint of Oneworld Publications, 2023

ISBN 978-0-86154-596-4
eISBN 978-0-86154-597-1

Typeset by Geethik Technologies
Printed and bound in Great Britain by Clays Ltd, Elcograf S.p.A.

Oneworld Publications
10 Bloomsbury Street, London WC1B 3SR, England

Stay up to date with the latest books,
special offers, and exclusive content from
Rock the Boat with our newsletter

Sign up on our website
rocktheboatbooks.com

For my niece, Jessica Bell.
I hope you enjoy reading this book one day.

Chapter 1

Bess Harper gritted her teeth, determined not to cry as she walked up the steps to the front doors of Harper's Odditorium. Even the whispering flowers adorning the walls of the building were shedding their dark petals as if in mourning and murmuring sadly to themselves. Bess loved Grandfather Henry and his peculiar museum, and now it seemed she would lose both in the space of a single week. She couldn't bear the thought that she would never again curl up beside Pops on the battered sofa in his study, listening to tales of his travels and adventures.

As if that weren't bad enough, Bess's dad and her Uncle Norman were sure to inherit the Odditorium and they intended to sell off the exhibits and close its doors forever. For some reason, Uncle Norman really seemed to hate the place. And her dad was a quiet man with no interest in strange museums and no desire to quarrel with his older brother.

"It's just a pile of old junk," Uncle Norman had said when he'd come to dinner the night before. "It ought to have been scrapped years ago."

"What about Blizzard?" Bess asked. "The Odditorium is his home!"

"We'll find another home for him."

"But you're always saying he's a horrible beast that no one in their right mind would want!" Bess protested. "What if he goes to someone who doesn't treat him properly? Someone who doesn't understand him?"

"Bess, please. You're giving me a headache." Uncle Norman let out a weary sigh. "You can rest assured that we'll find a home for him in a zoo somewhere. That's where he ought to have been all along. My father had no business keeping a creature like that in the Odditorium."

Bess later overheard Uncle Norman telling her parents that he'd tried calling a couple of zoos, but they were both full. So he had phoned the local glue factory instead and now poor old Blizzard was due to be shipped off and turned into glue sticks. That was her uncle's plan at any rate, but it wasn't *Bess's* plan.

The grown-ups were visiting the Odditorium today to meet her grandfather's lawyer and hear the reading of the will. They had agreed Bess could tag along, so that morning she'd thrown on her favourite Bigfoot T-shirt (for luck), tied her frizzy brown hair into two plaits (for convenience) and given herself an encouraging smile in the bathroom mirror (for courage).

Certainly no one else was going to encourage her with what she had in mind. Her rescue plan was dangerous, desperate and really not at all sensible, but it was also her only chance. When Bess smiled, it made her freckles more pronounced against her white skin. This reminded her of her grandfather and strengthened her determination. She took a deep breath and nodded at her reflection. She could do this. She had to. For Blizzard – and all the other exhibits.

By the time she got to the Odditorium, Uncle Norman and the lawyer were already there. Bess knew she wouldn't have long. She left her parents in the study with the other two and darted down the dusty corridor.

When it was originally built, some fifty years ago, the museum had been a grand mansion. Henry Harper had designed it himself, which was why it had a pleasing number of secret passages and spiral staircases hidden behind sliding bookshelves and paintings. Bess made her way to one of these secret passages now, grateful for the short cut it provided to the other side of the museum.

Uncle Norman and Bess's dad had both grown up here with their father and their mother, Lucy, who had passed away before Bess was born. The building hadn't been an Odditorium back then of course, but Pops had already been working on filling the rooms.

He'd often entertain Bess with accounts of his early quests for strange and interesting objects. Bess was never quite sure how much of this was truth and how much was fiction. Pops refused to speak about the years before he came to Roseville, including the family he'd left behind. Bess's dad and uncle had never met their grandparents. Nobody knew how Pops had made so much money either – enough to build this very mansion. Bess liked to think he'd been a jewel thief or something equally thrilling.

From the outside, the Odditorium still looked like a house with its pillars and balconies. For as long as Bess could remember, the walls had been covered in whispering flowers, their black petals edged with dark purple and dusky red. Henry had loved the flowers, but most people were wary of them because of all the teeth – sharp little rows nestled in the centre of the petals. The whispering flowers had never bitten anyone that Bess was aware of, but she'd always had the feeling that one day they just *might*.

They whispered non-stop, day and night, and sometimes you could glimpse the small dark flicker of a tongue within the petals. It was impossible to tell what they whispered about – although Bess had often strained her ears trying – because they all spoke different things at different times, creating a murmuring hush of sound.

Beyond the front doors, the Odditorium was transformed from the home it had once been. After the boys had grown up and moved out and Lucy had died, Henry expanded his collections until they filled most of the rooms. Then one day he decided to open his doors to the public, and nothing had been the same since.

The museum could certainly do with a good clean and a spruce-up. It had been closed for over a month, ever since Pops fell ill. There was only a handful of staff and they'd been let go when the Odditorium closed. All except Jamie, the caretaker, who'd been coming in twice a day to feed Blizzard, water the whispering flowers and check that Jessie the haunted doll wasn't causing too much havoc.

Jamie was a very old friend of Bess's grandfather and had worked at the Odditorium ever since it first opened. He knew how to handle all the exhibits safely and had done an excellent job of looking after the place, but it had still been hard for Bess not to be allowed to go there herself. At least she'd been permitted to visit Pops in the hospital, but it had seemed so wrong seeing him there, surrounded by white sheets and beeping machines. He belonged in the Odditorium with all his beloved books and fascinating objects.

She was glad to be back at last, although it was strange to find the museum deserted. Usually there were a few people wandering about, inspecting the curiosities or gazing up at the gigantic whale skeleton suspended from the lobby ceiling. But, when Bess emerged from the secret passage into a corridor, there wasn't a soul around. Motes of dust danced in the beams of light slanting through the large windows and there were several impressive spiderwebs spun round the chandeliers too. Bess was relieved that she could still make out the Odditorium's distinctive smell, her favourite scent in the whole world – a mixture of wax, maps and yellowed old bones.

Her footsteps echoed loudly as she hurried down the corridor, glancing into various rooms along the way. She wished she had time to rescue some of her other favourite exhibits – the mechanical fortune-teller, the complete set of elephant armour or the taxidermy specimen of a two-headed cat. But she would need every moment for Blizzard today. He was quite old now and moved about at a painfully slow speed – when he deigned to move at all.

She soon reached Blizzard's room at the end of the corridor. It was locked, as expected, but that wouldn't stop Bess for long. Pops had taught her many skills, some of which her parents knew about – such as map-reading – and others that she and Pops had kept secret. Bess's parents had no idea she knew how to charm a snake or catch a haunted doll, and they certainly hadn't a clue that she was an expert at lock-picking. She'd become even better at it than Pops in the end.

A few months ago, on her eleventh birthday, he'd given her a secret present – a little leather pouch filled with lock-picking equipment. There was a message inscribed on the inside of the flap:

For my darling Bess,

May you find great adventures behind any door you choose.

Love and mischief,
Pops xxxx

Bess never went anywhere without it and it took her less than a minute to get through the door. Back when the museum had been a mansion, this had been the ballroom. Uncle Norman always complained it was yet another example of Pops's eccentricity that he'd built such a lavish mansion for a family of four. Bess got the impression that her uncle and dad would both have preferred an ordinary home like their friends'. But Bess thought ordinary was overrated.

It took her eyes a moment to adjust to the murky darkness. The tall windows were lined with heavy wooden shutters because Blizzard was sensitive to light. The smell was just the same as always – swampy water mixed with a tang of bony fish and musty damp. Traces of the ballroom's previous use still remained in the cobwebbed chandelier hanging from the ceiling and the pale blue marble floor. When Pops had been younger and Lucy was still alive, they'd thrown lavish Christmas parties and invited the whole town. There hadn't been a swamp inside the ballroom back then of course.

The Odditorium had many large rooms, but the ballroom was the only one big enough to house Blizzard's immense tank. It took up almost the entire floor and contained an artificial swamp as well as a beach lined with glowing red heat lamps. There were several trees spread throughout the massive space, with long tendrils of hanging moss trailing down from their branches. In years gone by, visitors had sometimes complained that the darkness and the dense vegetation made it difficult to see inside the tank properly, but Pops had always insisted that an animal's comfort must come first.

Blizzard was much easier to spot nowadays though. At almost sixty years old, he spent most of his time basking beneath the heat lamps. Bess very much hoped this would be the case today as she ran up the curved staircase to the viewing platform. She peered over the side of the tank and, to her relief, there Blizzard was, stretched out upon the sand, snoring softly.

Bess paused for a moment to marvel at him. She didn't care what her uncle said – she thought he was spectacular. After all, it wasn't every day you got to stand so close to a three-metre-long white alligator.

Chapter 2

Pops had had strict rules about putting animals in the Odditorium. He would never remove anything from the wild if it was able to flourish there. But if a creature wasn't safe in its natural habitat for some reason, then he would consider rescuing it and providing a home at the Odditorium. He'd taken Blizzard in when the alligator had been just a hatchling. It seemed that someone had purchased him as a pet before thinking better of the idea and flushing him down the toilet. Pops had found him during one of his walkabouts through the sewers.

"People dispose of all kinds of unwanted and fascinating things that way," he'd told Bess. "That's why I like to have a browse down there from time to time."

Albino gators couldn't survive in the wild because their colouring meant they would be attacked by predators when they were small or else their delicate skin would get burned by the sun.

Bess had always adored Blizzard, but she knew full well he didn't feel the same way about her.

"You're just a walking snack as far as he's concerned," Pops had warned her quite cheerfully. "That's why you must always be very careful around his tank. Absolutely no messing about in the ballroom. Do all the messing about you like in the other rooms, but safety first when it comes to alligators, my dear. He'd happily gobble you up given half the chance, and that would be a very difficult thing to explain to your parents."

Blizzard was rare and beautiful, but he was also deadly. After all, he was basically a dinosaur and his alligator nature meant he wasn't capable of showing affection to anyone or anything – except perhaps his heat lamps. But he was now old and slow, and Bess had seen her grandfather put on his muzzle a couple of times when he needed to be moved from his tank in order for it to be cleaned. She was pretty confident she could do the same thing herself. At least she *hoped* she could. It didn't seem like there was any other option if she wanted to save Blizzard from his unhappy fate.

She turned to the cupboard on the balcony, entered the combination code and rummaged around inside until she found the key to Blizzard's tank, along with his muzzle and lead. They were made of strong leather, which was more than sufficient since all an alligator's biting strength is contained in the act of closing its mouth, not opening it. Bess had read once that a simple elastic band would be enough to keep a gator's jaw shut. She wouldn't like to test that theory, but she'd seen the muzzle in use enough times to know that it was up to the job.

Time was ticking on and she didn't know exactly how long she had left before the grown-ups came to find her and marched her out of the Odditorium forever. So she ran back down the stairs, draped the leather lead across her shoulders and unlocked the door of the tank. Taking her courage in both hands, she stepped inside.

Blizzard was still snoozing so this was her best chance of getting the muzzle on him without losing a finger. She held her breath and tiptoed over the sand. To her relief, Blizzard stayed snoring as she slipped the muzzle over his long head. She was just able to fasten the buckles before he opened one pink eye to stare lazily at her.

He blinked his eye shut, trying to go back to sleep, but Bess was having none of that. She tugged and heaved at the lead with all her might until the huge creature finally lumbered to his feet with a huff of irritation.

Blizzard slunk along beside her obediently enough as they entered the corridor, probably anticipating a dead rabbit as a reward. Bess's heart began to lift. The plan was working! Just a short distance away was the entrance to the sewers, hidden behind a large painting which swung open like a door. Pops had once shown her the spiral staircase behind the wall and told her how he used it to get into the underground tunnels whenever he fancied a poke around down there.

Bess had asked if she could go with him, but he'd shaken his head. "When you're older perhaps. I'll take you then."

But now Pops was gone and they'd never get the chance to explore down there together. The sewers were the only place Bess could think of that would be dark and wet enough for Blizzard. And there'd be no people to scream at the sight of him down there either. He'd have to catch his own food of course, but she hoped he'd be able to manage. If nothing else, it was better than him ending his days as a pile of glue sticks.

She was almost at the hidden entrance when a door banged somewhere behind her. "Bess! What on earth are you doing?" a voice exclaimed.

Her heart sank into her boots as she slowly turned round to face her uncle.

"Good Lord!" he said, staring at her with a horrified expression. "Is that the *alligator*? What are you thinking of? Take him back to wherever he's supposed to be at once!"

Bess tightened her grip on Blizzard's lead and firmly planted her feet, determined not to be bullied. "I overheard you on the phone," she said. "And I won't let you sell Blizzard to the glue factory. I won't."

Uncle Norman shook his head and straightened his tie. It was a gesture he often made whenever he was irritated, which seemed to be most of the time.

"Sell him?" he replied in a scornful tone. "You must be joking. No one wants a beast like that. I was going to give him away. I'd have paid them to take him off my hands frankly, but never mind that now. I've been looking all over this blasted place for you. We've been talking to the lawyer and it seems there's been a terrible mistake. Your father and I haven't inherited the museum after all."

"What?" Bess felt a flash of hope. Perhaps the new person wouldn't feel the same way as her uncle and there might be a chance for the Odditorium. "Who's the owner then?"

Uncle Norman's mouth tightened and he straightened his tie again. "You are."

He then reached into his pocket and uncurled his fingers to reveal a shining golden key lying in the palm of his hand.

Chapter 3

At first, it seemed Bess's problems were solved. She would keep the exhibits safe – including Blizzard – open the Odditorium once more and everything would be all right.

Only it wasn't quite that simple. When the weekend arrived and Bess flipped the sign on the door to OPEN, there was no rush of excited visitors like she'd been expecting. In fact, the Odditorium was open for three whole hours before anyone walked inside. Even then it was only a confused lady who had got lost and was looking for the hat shop. To make matters worse, Jamie wasn't around to help her. He'd left a note on Pops's desk saying that the whispering flowers had run out of food and he'd gone to look for some. Bess thought he'd probably be back within an hour, but he was away all weekend.

She set off for home on Sunday evening feeling thoroughly dejected. She lived with her parents in a small, tidy, extremely ordinary house. There was nothing unusual about it at all, except perhaps for the fact that it had rather a lot of flowers. There were floral patterns on the wallpaper, painted daisies on the china, rose prints on the bedsheets and so on. Bess thought that a cursed mirror or a sabre-toothed tiger skull would improve the place immensely.

Almost everyone in Roseville was keen on flowers of course since the small town was known for its impressive rose garden. It was located opposite the Odditorium and was famous for its special roses that bloomed all year round. A large team of gardeners looked after it, including Bess's parents.

Mr and Mrs Harper didn't hate the Odditorium in the way that Uncle Norman did, but they didn't love it either. Bess's parents had no desire to be amazed and astounded. They just wanted to have a nice early tea round the kitchen table, then perhaps do a jigsaw puzzle before taking a lukewarm bath and going to bed.

"Sometimes things skip a generation and that's what happened with your uncle and dad," Pops had told Bess. "I thought there might be a glimmer of hope for your father once, long ago, but now I realise that neither of them has got an adventurous bone in their body. I imagine they'd both be quite happy to spend the rest of their lives in Roseville."

It was the closest he'd ever got to talking about his own parents. That and telling Bess that their family had always had green fingers. Even Uncle Norman owned a cactus collection he was rather proud of. And Bess had her own unique skills when it came to gardening too, only her speciality involved something more interesting than flowers.

After another disappointing day at the Odditorium, Bess found the sight of all the roses on the dining-room wallpaper even more depressing than usual. To make matters worse, Uncle Norman had come for tea.

"Business isn't exactly booming at the Odditorium from what I hear," he said the moment they sat down at the table. He looked extremely pleased by this. "I'm not surprised. Visitors have been dwindling at that mouldy old place for years."

"There is no mould," Bess replied, spearing a carrot on her plate with rather more force than was necessary. "Just dust and cobwebs."

"People weren't coming any more even before Father fell ill," Uncle Norman went on as if Bess hadn't spoken.

"I'm afraid that's true," Bess's dad said, although at least he looked regretful. "The thing is, not everyone is…well, quite so fond of odd things as you are, Bess. Most folk around here would rather spend their free time taking a stroll through the rose garden or painting pots at the pottery café or some such."

Bess pulled a face. What was the matter with people? How could anyone possibly prefer painting pots to looking at an albino alligator or a haunted doll? She shook her head in despair.

"Well, I think those people are silly," she said. "And if they don't want to come to the Odditorium then it's their loss."

"Actually," Uncle Norman said with a horrible smile, "I think you'll find it's very much *your* loss, *Elizabeth*."

Bess winced. Her uncle was the only person who ever called her Elizabeth, probably because he knew how much she disliked it.

"The Odditorium can't run on air," Uncle Norman went on in a self-satisfied tone. "There are bills to be paid and expenses to be met. The caretaker will expect to receive wages. If you can't get the place to pay for itself, then you'll have no choice but to sell it. I give it a few weeks – a couple of months tops – and then the Odditorium will be out of business. And good riddance. It's been a burden and an embarrassment to our family for too long."

Bess stood up from the table. "It's not an embarrassment to *me*," she said, feeling hot and angry. "I'm proud of what Pops created. I love it there."

Uncle Norman looked expectantly at her parents, waiting for them to scold Bess for answering back, but they were both intent on examining the daisy-patterned plates before them.

"Well, that," her uncle said coldly, "is why you have very few friends at school from what I understand."

Bess gave a sharp intake of breath and felt a flush of shame prickle over her skin. She'd only really ever had one proper friend – a curly-haired girl called Milly. They'd been as close as sisters in infant school, but as soon as they moved up to juniors Milly formed friendships with a couple of other girls – Olivia and Kayleigh. These new friends definitely weren't into haunted dolls and albino alligators. They liked unicorns instead.

They'd even formed their own Unicorn Club – one that Bess was absolutely not allowed to join. Not that she wanted to. There were too many rainbow tails and sparkles for her liking. But she still missed Milly sometimes. And no one likes eating their sandwiches by themselves at lunch and having no one to partner with in class. It mortified Bess that her parents had mentioned her friendless state to her uncle of all people.

"Norman!" her dad snapped with a rare show of irritation. "That's quite enough!"

But Uncle Norman was already gathering up his things to leave. "If you'll excuse me," he said, "I think I've lost my appetite." A moment later, he was on his way, the door banging shut behind him.

"He may be my brother, but he can be a singularly unpleasant person sometimes," Mr Harper said with a sigh.

"No arguments here," Mrs Harper said, looking equally exasperated. "Don't pay him any attention, Bess."

Uncle Norman might have been an unpleasant type, but sadly it turned out that he was right about the bills. Bess found stacks and stacks of them in her grandfather's study when she visited the Odditorium after school the next day. Jamie had obviously returned from wherever he'd gone to because there was a new note from him on the desk telling her that the whispering flowers needed food URGENTLY.

Bess shook her head and moved the note to one side. The flowers would have to wait – there were more important matters to attend to. She felt like a bit of a snoop as she started to go through Pops's desk, but everything in it belonged to her now after all, and she needed to start cataloguing and organising things.

She was also half hoping to find a map that she'd once seen lying on the desk. It had been old and yellowed, the thick parchment curling at the edges. And it had featured names that Bess had recognised from her storybooks. Places like Cinderella's Palace, Snow White's Forest, Jack's Beanstalk and the Evil Queen's Castle. Bess could still picture the vibrant red apples and the golden gleam of spinning wheels painted in the margins.

She had only got a brief glimpse before Pops had snatched the map away. Usually he was keen to explain where various items came from, but he'd shoved it into one of the desk drawers and refused to answer any questions about it. This had piqued Bess's curiosity and she'd always wondered about that map, but now she couldn't find it anywhere.

Bess let out a sigh as she added another bill to the pile. Somehow or other she needed to find money for electricity, wages and rabbits for Blizzard. The whispering flowers still looked sickly and Bess's poisoned-apple tree was in a bad way too, according to Jamie. The caretaker had done the best he could with it, he'd said, but it was very particular. Now that she was here, Bess decided she ought to go and check on it herself. She left the study and went down the corridor to the room where the tree was on display.

Pops had said that Bess was the only person he'd ever known who had managed to grow one. A few years ago she'd picked up a sprig of apple blossom in her garden and decided to have a go at pressing it. She'd seen her mum do this with roses and thought there was something quite interesting about putting a specimen between the pages of a large, heavy book until it dried out. A flower could be kept for a hundred years or more that way.

She'd taken the blossom into her house and found the largest book she owned – a hardback volume of fairy tales. She then tucked some newspaper into the book and carefully pressed the blossom inside. The first time she'd checked on her specimen she'd been in for a shock. Instead of a single dried blossom, an entire miniature tree had unfolded from within the pages. Its roots were wrapped round the spine of the book and apples the size of marbles hung from the branches, startlingly red.

When she'd shown it to Pops, he'd told her it was a very difficult thing to press a tree, something even the most skilled botanists struggled to achieve. And it seemed to have soaked up some of the words from the fairy-tale book too, because it was no longer an ordinary tree but a poisoned-apple one.

"Where did you get that book anyway?" Pops had asked. He'd looked disapproving, which was odd because Pops normally loved books.

"Mum bought it, I think. Why?"

Pops had sniffed and given the book a disdainful look. "I don't much care for fairy tales, that's all. They only tell one side of the story."

Pops had gone on to explain to Bess that there were several different types of poisoned-apple tree. There were ones to make a person fall asleep, ones to make them lose all their memories and ones – like Bess's tree – to make a person tell the truth.

"The apple blossom is interesting too," he'd said. "The truth can be a dangerous thing of course, and so perhaps people are right to fear the apples. But truth is also knowledge and knowledge is a priceless gift. One sniff of the scented blossoms and you'll be gifted with the knowledge of a fact you didn't know before."

When Bess had asked how Pops knew so much about poisoned apples, he'd laughed and tickled her under the chin. "I know many things about many things, dear one. You should know that by now."

He was certainly right about the apple blossoms. Bess had learned a lot of interesting titbits from them over the years – including that it's impossible for a pig to look up at the sky and that lobsters pee from their faces. You sniffed the blossom and the fact just appeared in your head as if someone had spoken the words aloud.

With Bess's permission, Grandfather Henry had put the pressed tree on display in the Odditorium, but now she was dismayed to see that its leaves were drooping sadly and it didn't have a single apple. She carefully closed the book, the tree folding itself up neatly between the covers, and decided to take it home. Nobody would miss a lone exhibit and she could better nurse it back to health if it was enjoying the company of her other pressed trees.

Bess had done several more since that first one and had quite the miniature forest on the bookshelves of her bedroom. She'd experimented with using blossom, leaves, fruit and even pieces of root, and was fascinated by the way the book itself had an impact on the specimen. A volume of spooky stories had produced a bone-white ghost tree with spectral branches, while a dictionary had created a tree made up of words – some of which Bess had never even heard of. One of Bess's favourite pressed trees came from a book about the ocean, which had grown a tree made of coral and covered in tiny starfish.

Bess wondered now whether some of these trees might make good exhibits for the Odditorium. She needed to get visitors in and fast. Perhaps people didn't realise it was open again. On returning home, Bess had just enough time before bed to draw up some flyers to hand out the next day. Then she fell into a restless sleep.

The following morning Bess went straight to the rose garden to hand out her flyers. But she quickly discovered that the inhabitants of the town didn't much care whether the Odditorium was open or not.

"That old place?" one smartly dressed woman remarked. "I thought it had closed down years ago."

"Oh no, we're still open!" Bess hurried to reassure her. "And we've got all kinds of fascinating creatures to see, curiosities to inspect and—"

"That may be, but once you've seen them you've seen them," the woman interrupted. "And everyone knows that the Odditorium hasn't had anything new on display for years."

Bess was baffled. Personally she'd never get tired of looking at Blizzard, let alone all the other awesome things in the museum.

"Perhaps if you were to improve your facilities?" one cheerful man suggested. "I mean, there isn't even a café or a giftshop. It would be nice to be able to buy a tea towel or a magnet or something."

Bess had always thought that the Odditorium could do with both a giftshop and a café – maybe an ice-cream parlour with extraordinary flavours and spectacular sprinkles. She had lots of ideas, but she couldn't carry out a single one without money. And right now she still had no idea how to get her hands on any.

She trudged back to the Odditorium, but on reaching it she stopped short in horror. The whispering flowers normally clung to the walls, but during the night their vines had broken through the windows and reached into the museum itself. Not only that, but Bess could see chunks of brick and plaster on the ground where the flowers had chipped bits away from the building.

Pops had told Bess that the whispering flowers could be dangerous, but she'd thought he meant because of their teeth. She'd never imagined they might be a threat to the Odditorium itself. She hurried inside only to find that the flowers were everywhere. Their whispering had taken on an urgent, frantic sort of tone, although Bess still couldn't make out any individual words.

Much of the ground floor was already scattered with broken glass and wilting dark petals, and when Bess walked into one of the rooms at the back of the Odditorium, she saw vines reaching in through the broken window, creeping along the ceiling before her eyes. Within minutes, the room was a forest of flowers so dense that Bess couldn't even find her way back to the door.

Chapter 4

Bess scrambled out of the window and ran round to the front doors. She hurried from room to room, searching for Jamie. He was a small, wiry man in his seventies who had always had a kind word for Bess growing up or a sugar toad for her in his pocket. She'd wondered where he got the sweets because the local shop only stocked sugar mice. There was something wrong with one of his hands, but Bess wasn't quite sure what as he always wore gloves, even in the summer.

She liked him very much and found it especially comforting to be around him now because it felt like he was the only other person who missed Pops as much as she did. He was certainly the only other person who cared about the fate of the Odditorium.

When she finally tracked him down, he was kneeling on the ground, fixing a leaking pipe on the first floor.

He wore his usual uniform of blue overalls and his white hair stuck out in random directions as always. Bess could see that a whispering flower had grown straight through the pipe, cracking the metal. She dreaded to think how much it might cost to repair all this damage.

"What's happening?" she gasped. "Why are the flowers attacking the museum?"

Jamie looked up and wiped his hand across his forehead, leaving behind a streak of grease. "They're hungry, miss. They're not attacking the place – they're just looking for food. We ran out a few days ago. Didn't you get my note?"

"Well, yes, but don't the flowers just need sunlight and water? And beans obviously?"

About once a month, Bess would see Jamie going from flower to flower with a sack in his hands. He'd take the beans out one at a time and toss them to the flowers to avoid getting his fingers bitten. Bess had never given it much thought. She'd always assumed the beans just came from the local grocer's.

Jamie cleared his throat. "There's a bit more to it than that. Didn't your pops ever tell you anything about the flowers?"

"He said they could be dangerous," Bess replied. "But so are lots of things in the Odditorium."

The caretaker stood up and wiped his hands on a rag. "When it comes to the whispering flowers, there are certain things that aren't for me to say. Either your pops wanted you to know or he didn't. I won't interfere with that. But I can tell you that they need three things." He ticked them off on his fingers. "Water, moonlight and magic beans."

Bess gaped at him. "*Magic* beans? You mean like in *Jack and the Beanstalk*?"

Jamie shrugged.

"Where am I supposed to get those from?" Bess asked.

"Beats me. Henry always bought them. They come in a sack about this big."

He gestured with his hands, but Bess was at a loss. She couldn't exactly pop down to her local supermarket for such a thing.

Over the following days, she searched the Odditorium from top to bottom, but there wasn't a single sack of magic beans to be found. In desperation, she thought of the secret door leading to the sewers.

It seemed unlikely that Pops would have hidden beans down there. His descriptions had made it sound dark and damp, and hardly a good place for storing anything, much less food. But Bess didn't want to leave any stone unturned and she'd been meaning to explore the tunnels anyway. So one afternoon, on her way home from school, she donned her wellies, slipped a torch into her pocket and pressed the button in the painting's frame to reveal the door Pops had shown her.

The moment it slid open, the sconces on the walls lit up, providing enough light for Bess to see by. She lost no time descending the spiral staircase, keeping one hand on the railing built into the wall. Before long, she reached the bottom and another series of lights switched on, illuminating the tunnel up ahead.

Bess stared around in surprise. She'd expected to be ankle-deep in sewage by now and had been preparing herself for a truly horrible smell, but the tunnel stretching before her wasn't a sewer at all. It was a train tunnel. Bess could see lines of tracks disappearing into the shadows and she was standing on a station platform.

It was quite a fancy one in fact, considering it was tucked underground where no one was ever likely to see it. The walls were covered in bottle-green bricks that gleamed handsomely in the lamplight and a sign on the wall announced the destination: HARPER'S

ODDITORIUM. There was a black wrought-iron bench to sit on, a clock upon the wall and a barrier with a ticket machine, separating one part of the platform from the other.

Bess stared. Pops had always been very clear that there was nothing but sewer tunnels down here. Why had he lied?

She walked over to get a closer look at the ticket machine. Of course she had no ticket to insert and she could easily climb over the barrier if she wanted to anyway. There didn't seem to be much point though because the platform was quite empty. There were definitely no sacks of magic beans lying conveniently around.

Once she was sure she couldn't hear any trains approaching, Bess hopped down on to the tracks and walked a little way along the tunnel, shining her torch this way and that. But there was nothing to see except for the occasional rat scrabbling in the shadows.

Bess had no idea what these tunnels were for. She'd never heard about any underground train tunnels in Roseville and could only assume that this must be some relic from the town's past. She didn't imagine any trains could possibly run down here these days. And she still couldn't think why Pops had told her there were nothing but sewers down here. What could he have been trying to hide?

Bess had planned to go back down there the following day and explore the tunnels properly, but then Uncle Norman found out about the whispering flowers. He promptly reported her to the town council and, before she knew it, Bess had been served with an official notice saying that the flowers were in breach of regulations and posed a hazard to health and safety. She was instructed to close her doors with immediate effect; if she couldn't get the flowers under control by the end of the month, the council would issue a further notice to demolish the building.

"Oh, Jessie, I'm stuck!" Bess exclaimed, slumping down on the floor in front of Jessie's cabinet.

Jessie was a porcelain doll with innocent blue eyes, blonde ringlets and a fetching lace bonnet. She looked lovely, but the truth was that she'd stick a pin straight into your hand given half the chance, and she'd enjoy doing it too. In the end, Pops had had to put a little bit of sticky tape over her mouth to stop her from telling children to set things on fire. Jessie probably didn't have any experience of trying to make money or locating magic beans, but Bess found herself talking to her anyway.

"I need to get magic beans from somewhere, but I have to go to school. I can't just set off on an adventure whenever I feel like it, like Pops did when he was collecting things for the museum. I don't even know where he got the magic beans from! It might be somewhere halfway across the world. What am I supposed to do? I can't let them demolish the Odditorium, I just can't! Especially not after Pops put his trust in me."

A light tapping made her jump and she looked up to see Jessie knocking her porcelain fingertips delicately against the glass. Bess was surprised – and rather honoured – that Jessie would move in front of her. Normally the doll only did that when no one was watching.

"What is it?" she asked, standing up and stepping closer.

The doll pointed insistently at her mouth, so Bess fumbled through her big ring of keys until she found the one for Jessie's case.

Bess paused. "Do you promise not to poke me with a pin if I unlock this?"

Jessie blinked her innocent blue eyes and nodded once. Bess opened the cabinet and reached in to pull the sticky tape from Jessie's lips.

"Do you have an idea?" she asked hopefully. "A way to save the Odditorium?"

The doll leaned forward slightly. "Burn it down!" she hissed in a high-pitched little voice. "Burn it all down!" Then she jabbed Bess with the pin that had suddenly appeared in her tiny porcelain hand.

Bess sighed. "Thanks, Jessie. That's no help to me at all."

She bundled the doll up, replaced the tape and stuffed her back in her case. In the process, an envelope slipped out from between Jessie's petticoats and landed on the floor. Bess quickly locked the door and looked down at it. To her surprise, her own name was written on the front in Pops's handwriting. She snatched the envelope up and tore it open.

Her eager fingers pulled out a letter written on thick, creamy paper. Tucked within was a shining golden ticket. It had dark edges and was stamped with a picture of a steam train. Beneath this were printed the words: ADMITS ONE. Bess stared at the ticket, thinking of the underground station she'd found. Then she turned her attention to the letter itself. It was dated just before Pops went into hospital. Her heart beat a little faster as she scanned down the page.

My dearest Bess,

If you're reading this, then it most likely means I'm no longer here. I hope of course to recover – there are always more adventures to be had – but something tells me I may not come home from this hospital visit. Please try not to be too sad. I've lived a life filled with escapades and there isn't much I would change if I could do it all over again.

Now I expect you're already aware that you're the new owner of the Odditorium and I know you will do great things with the place. I imagine it seems a little peculiar for me to have entrusted this message to Jessie, but you're the only person brave enough to take her out of her case, and if I'd given this letter to my lawyer then I've no doubt Norman would have managed to get his greedy fingers on it.

We don't want a stuffy old windbag like him poking his nose in — this is private Odditorium business, from one owner to another.

My dear, there is much you will learn about the exhibits as time goes by, but one thing you must know is that the whispering flowers are the most important item in the whole museum and they require magical food (about once a month) to flourish. They have an especial preference for magic beans, but anything magical will do as long as it requires some chewing. They like using their teeth, you see. They got quite irate when I offered them a magic smoothie once — I think they felt that slurping food up through a straw was beneath them.

Since I can't show you where to get the magic beans from, I suggest that you seek out my faithful friend Professor Ash and his marvellous train. He will, I am sure, be happy to assist. I expect you've already ventured into the underground tunnels by now and have discovered the train station there. I longed to tell you all about it, but you'll find out for yourself soon enough why that was impossible. All you need do is feed the enclosed train ticket into the machine down there and the rest will follow.

My dear girl, I know you will have the most wonderful time aboard the Train of Dark Wonders. How I wish I could go on this adventure with you. Have fun – and do all the things I would most certainly do without hesitation! We only get one life and time is more precious than we can ever truly appreciate.

Much love and mischief,
Pops xxxx

PS If the professor is not immediately available, then feed the whispering flowers some of your poisoned apples. That should keep them going for a while.

Bess felt a mix of excitement and exasperation as she stared at the letter in her hand. She was thrilled at the thought of a mysterious train, but still didn't understand the secrecy. Her thoughts turned to the pressed tree back home, its branches drooping, leaves wilting, not sporting so much as a single apple. Pops's advice that she feed the whispering flowers the apples was all very well, but how could she bring the tree back to life?

"It's like it knows you're sad," her mum had said the other day. "And it's sharing your grief."

If that was the problem, then Bess didn't know what she could do to fix it. Grief wasn't exactly an emotion that could be switched on and off. Still, at least she could give the train ticket a try.

Bess lost no time returning through the secret door to the underground platform. She held the ticket to the slot and machinery whirred into life within, sucking it in immediately. But then…nothing.

She waited, wondering if something had gone wrong. Perhaps the machine was broken? She gave it a tentative thump. The thing seemed to have simply eaten her ticket. Bess tried to control her rising frustration.

Eventually she was forced to give up and return to the Odditorium, but even that wasn't straightforward. A tangle of whispering flowers had grown over the secret door, jamming it shut, and Bess had to throw her shoulder against it in order to force a gap large enough to squeeze through. The museum was being taken over by the flowers, weeping their petals on to the floor, and Bess had no idea how to find this Professor Ash person or his train.

Chapter 5

There was little time to think about Professor Ash or the Train of Dark Wonders over the next few days – Bess was too busy trying to protect the museum's exhibits. She didn't think the whispering flowers necessarily meant to damage things, but by now the vines were twisting and growing through almost every room. That meant that display cases were prone to getting knocked over and broken, and some of the Odditorium's more delicate items were at risk.

With Jamie's help, she'd managed to barricade the ballroom by boarding up the windows and doors. The last thing they needed was for the flowers to break Blizzard's tank, leaving him free to roam the corridors.

Once the alligator was taken care of, they turned their attention to securing the upstairs rooms. Bess spent every day after school moving the fragile exhibits up there one at a time. Her arms ached and she'd sneezed over and over again with the dust, but finally there was only the doll's house still to go. Bess tottered under its weight, barely managing to keep her footing on the stairs. With relief, she finally set it down in one of the safe rooms.

The doll's house was an abandoned, foreboding sort of structure and the entire front opened to reveal the rooms within. It had clearly once been very grand, but now the tiny chandeliers were covered in cobwebs, the windows were broken and the wallpaper was peeling.

Pops had suspected that there'd once been some kind of haunting in the little house judging by the amount of miniature Ouija boards, tiny tarot cards and fortune-telling teacups scattered throughout the rooms. Even the larder was full of small glass bottles labelled *ghost pepper* – a substance that was meant to be able to banish ghosts.

Bess thought the bottles were rather pretty and with Pops's permission had strung one of them on to a necklace, along with a couple of pearls and a bead shaped like a bat. She wore it all the time, despite the fact that Milly and the other Unicorn Club girls teased her about it.

As she checked over the doll's house to make sure it was undamaged, Bess turned her attention to the tiny attic. There were lots of little trunks up there full of the dolls' belongings. Bess had never actually inspected the contents herself so she scooped up the trunks and dropped them into her backpack. She'd catalogue them in her bedroom after tea. Perhaps there'd be something interesting in one of them that she could put on display or even something that might help with the whispering flowers.

She'd tried asking Jamie about the flowers again just that morning, since he clearly knew more about them than he was willing to say. But he'd clammed up immediately, only repeating that he didn't know where to get the magic beans from. As for the Train of Dark Wonders and Professor Ash, he was curiously reluctant to discuss them either.

"Your pops went to a lot of strange places and met a lot of strange folk," he'd said. "That was his affair. Some of us just want a quiet life of minding our own business."

"But did you know about the train tunnels under the museum?" Bess pressed.

"Course I knew," Jamie replied. "You wouldn't catch me down there though. Some things are best left well alone in my humble opinion."

Try as she might, Bess couldn't get anything further out of him. Feeling rather defeated, she swung the bag on to her back and walked to the entrance, intending to return home for tea. But when she opened the front doors she found quite a crowd had gathered outside and they were all staring at the rose garden.

From her position on the museum steps, Bess had a good view over everyone's heads and she saw that there was a puppet, about half a metre tall, standing beneath the garden's gated archway. She could tell by the fact that he wore a black frock coat, a red-lined cape and a bow tie that he was a magician. Beneath one arm he carried a top hat with a pair of little white bunny-rabbit ears poking out of the top.

Bess guessed the puppet was crafted from felt, although his hair and moustache seemed to be made from black fluff that stuck out at rather peculiar angles. But the strangest thing was that the puppet was moving about by himself. Bess couldn't see any strings or poles and there was no one standing anywhere nearby. The only possible explanation was that the puppet was magic in some way.

The puppet magician raised his arms with a flourish towards the roses and the crowd gasped. Bess realised he was enchanting the blooms somehow. With every sweep of his arm, the flowers in the bushes turned from their usual vibrant red into a black and white pattern. They had been transformed into paper. Several fell to the ground and someone picked one up and unfolded it to reveal a flyer.

She wasn't surprised when the crowd started tutting in disapproval – the citizens of Roseville were very proud and protective of their roses – but Bess thought it was one of the best magic displays she'd ever seen. Keen to get a closer look at the puppet, she quickly shut the Odditorium's doors and was just about to hurry down the steps when she heard a voice beside her.

"Oh, have you closed for the day? I was hoping to go inside."

Startled, Bess turned round to see a boy standing next to her. He was dressed in black from head to toe, and would almost have merged with the shadows if it weren't for his pale skin. His messy black hair reminded her of the puppet magician's and his right hand was moving busily at his side as if he were making an invisible puppet dance.

Bess glanced from the boy to the puppet beside the garden gates and back again. "Are you…controlling that?" she asked.

Down below, the tuts of complaint had turned into louder grumbles as people fretted over the roses and whether they'd been permanently changed into paper.

"How could I be?" the boy said with a cheerful grin. Bess couldn't help noticing that his blue eyes were full of mischief. "I'm nowhere near it. So are you then?" He peered over her shoulder at the museum. "Closed, I mean?"

"Yes," Bess said. "For now. We're… We're having a bit of a problem with our whispering flowers."

Indeed, the Odditorium was looking distinctly dilapidated with all its broken windows and chipped bits of plaster.

"That's a pity," the boy replied. "Perhaps some other time."

There suddenly came another gasp from the crowd and Bess saw that the magician had vanished.

"Oh bother!" she said. "I wanted to take a look at that puppet." She glanced back at the boy. "I don't suppose you know where he's gone?"

"No idea," he said with an innocent shrug, although Bess was pretty sure she saw a pair of white bunny ears poking out of his sleeve before he briskly adjusted the cuff. "But if you want to see more of him then come along tonight."

He handed her a paper rose that seemed to appear in his hand from nowhere. When Bess unfolded it, she saw that it was an invitation of some kind. Her breath caught in her throat as she read the words printed there.

PREPARE TO BE AMAZED
PREPARE TO BE EXCITED
PREPARE TO BE ASTOUNDED
AT THE TRAIN OF DARK WONDERS
FOR ONE NIGHT ONLY
ON ROSEVILLE'S TALLEST HILL

A tiny steam train was stamped into each of the flyer's four corners – identical to the one on Bess's ticket. The Train of Dark Wonders… She looked up to ask the boy some more questions, but he had gone, melting away into the shadows without a sound.

Bess was about to head down the steps to see if she could spot him on the street when the museum doors opened behind her and Jamie stepped out. His gaze fell on the flyer still clutched in her hand and he gave a grunt.

"About time that thing showed up. I suppose you'll go?"

"My parents won't want me to," Bess said.

Jamie grinned. "You're staying at home then of course." He locked the museum doors and slipped the key into his pocket. "Goodnight, young miss."

"Goodnight, Jamie. Thanks for helping me today."

He lifted a hand in acknowledgement and started to walk down the steps, but suddenly paused. "If you *do* happen to find yourself on the train, don't worry about the Odditorium. I can look after the old place while you're gone and keep the flowers in check until you get back."

Bess laughed. "The train's only at Roseville for one night. So, even if I did go to see it, I wouldn't be away for long."

Jamie glanced back over his shoulder. There was an expression on his face she found impossible to read. "We'll see," he said quietly.

Then he walked down the rest of the steps, leaving Bess alone.

ChAPTER 6

Bess stuffed the flyer into her pocket and hurried home as fast as she could, excitement thrumming through her veins. She didn't know how or why, but the Train of Dark Wonders was here and hopefully Professor Ash was too. Maybe he could help her find a way to save the Odditorium. She decided not to mention anything to her parents. She knew they wouldn't want her to go and there was absolutely no way she was going to miss this, not after Pops's letter. But her dad had seen one of the flyers while working in the rose garden and raised the subject at teatime.

"I really can't think why people would want to spend their Friday night going to such a place when they could be warm and cosy inside."

He looked genuinely baffled. Bess was sure that if she asked to visit the train then that familiar look of confused disappointment would appear on both her parents' faces. It was bad enough not fitting in at school, but it made Bess especially sad on those occasions when it felt like she didn't fit in very well at home either. She kept carefully silent, but this only seemed to rouse her parents' suspicion.

"Did you hear anything about this?" her mum asked, giving her a close look.

Bess shook her head. "I was busy in the Odditorium after school," she said. Thinking it might look odd if she didn't ask any questions, she added, "What kind of train is it?"

"Never mind," her dad replied. "It doesn't matter."

Bess stayed very still for the rest of the meal in case the flyer should rustle in her pocket.

Afterwards, she dutifully helped her mum with a one-thousand-piece jigsaw puzzle of a large bowl of fruit in the living room. It was hard to sit quietly when she was so thrilled about the train, but Bess did her best to act normally.

Finally, it was time to go to bed. Bess went upstairs, slipped her nightdress on over her jeans and Bigfoot T-shirt, then climbed under the duvet. When her mum came to give her a goodnight kiss a few minutes later, she made sure to yawn loudly and snuggle into her pillow as if she were already half asleep. But as soon as her mother left the room Bess sprang out of bed, threw off her nightie and tied up her hair into a ponytail.

She grabbed her backpack and was about to head for the window when she paused and turned back to scoop up the book containing the pressed poisoned-apple tree. She had the dolls' trunks, but it might be useful to have a more spectacular example from the Odditorium with her just in case she needed to prove that she was who she said she was. With the book stowed in her now much heavier bag, she headed for the window.

It was a crisp autumn evening. The air was cool and fresh and smelled of apples from the tree outside. Bess was an expert at using this to escape the house. She'd done it on more than one occasion to meet Pops at the Odditorium, back when he was teaching her how to read stars from the roof.

All the light had drained from the sky long ago, but she still kept low to the ground as she slunk through the garden. The last thing she wanted was for her parents to spot her. A few minutes later, she was hurrying down the road towards the tallest hill on the outskirts of Roseville. Clearly most of the town had heard about the train and there was quite a crowd making its way towards the spot. From the talk around her, Bess worked out that some people were excited to see the train while others were still annoyed about what had happened with the roses.

They arrived at the hill soon enough. It was quite steep and everyone stopped talking in order to save their breath for climbing up alongside the train tracks. Bess smelled the train before she saw it. Steam from the engine drifted down the hill towards them, carrying a host of other scents. Bess could detect hot dogs, popcorn and candyfloss, along with other less familiar things.

At last, they reached the top of the hill. The Train of Dark Wonders stood in all its glory directly ahead, resting on the tracks. Beside it, Bess could see stalls set out with red-and-white-striped awnings. It looked like some sort of funfair. There were lots of people milling about, buying sticks of candyfloss and winning prizes at the hook-a-duck stand.

Flickering lamps surrounded the train and Bess saw that there were six large carriages attached to the steam engine, all painted as black as night and speckled with silver stars. They shone smartly in the lamplight. Behind the train loomed the forest and it almost seemed as if the trees themselves leaned forward slightly, eager to see what was going on. Bess started heading for the train, but the smell from a nearby hot-dog stand was too tempting so she stopped to join the queue.

There was a performance taking place nearby. A man, woman and girl were all spinning flaming sticks in great arcs and loops, lighting up the night sky with vivid red streaks of fire.

Every now and then, the flames seemed to form shapes that made it look as if tiny red dragons were flying and swooping round them. Bess guessed the performers were a family because they all had the same long thin noses, brown skin and curly black hair. Their outfits matched, with a lot of black and red sequins.

The girl had bright red streaks in her hair. She looked about Bess's age and Bess couldn't help feeling a flicker of jealousy. How she wished that she could travel aboard a train of wonders, performing fire shows every night, rather than struggling through maths lessons that made her want to cry with boredom, to say nothing of the endless teasing for not looking the right way or saying the right things.

"Can I interest you in a hot frog, young lady?"

Bess had been so engrossed in the performance that she hadn't realised she'd reached the front of the queue.

"Oh yes, please." She turned towards the stallholder, who was dressed in an emerald green waistcoat. But halfway through reaching for her purse she froze. "Hot *frog*? Don't you mean hot dog?"

"Oh no." The man laughed. "There are no hot dogs served here."

Bess craned her neck, trying to get a better look over the counter. "Is it... Is it actually made from frog then?"

The man smiled. "Of course not! Hot dogs aren't made from dogs, are they?"

"Oh. No. I suppose not." Bess still couldn't see what was behind the counter, but she decided to be adventurous. "Okay, I'll have one hot frog then, please."

The man leaned over to hand Bess a bun with a bright green sausage inside. "Enjoy," he said with a grin.

Bess considered asking exactly what the sausage was made of, but then thought better of it and thanked him instead. "By the way, do you know that a mail train is due to come through here soon?" she added. "It'll travel over the hill at top speed and it won't be expecting your train to be blocking the tracks, so—"

The stallholder waved a hand. "Don't worry about that," he said. "Professor Ash always studies the train timetables in advance. We'll be gone by then. Best enjoy all this while you can."

"Where is Professor Ash?" Bess asked eagerly. "I need to speak to him."

"Good luck with that," the stallholder replied. "Professor Ash doesn't come out for the shows."

Bess wanted to ask more questions, but the stallholder was already calling the next customer forward so she carried her hot frog over to a bench and took a cautious bite. It tasted good – if a little swampy. She was just getting used to the taste when she spotted Milly and the other Unicorn Club girls walking past, all wearing matching rainbow skirts. They immediately noticed Bess sitting alone on the bench and giggled as they pointed her out.

A wave of hurt washed over Bess. She felt foolish on her own when everyone else was here with friends or family. If Pops were still alive, she knew he would have come with her and she suddenly felt his absence so strongly that she could almost see him sitting on the bench beside her, tucking into a hot frog and exclaiming in delight over its unusual flavour.

Milly said something to the other two, then they all let out peals of laughter before walking off. Bess realised she was clenching her jaw as she watched them go. She wasn't so bothered about Kayleigh and Olivia because they'd never been friends, but Milly had come to play at Bess's house many times. She'd even been to the Odditorium once – although it hadn't taken long before she was frightened by a mummified cat and started crying. But they *had* been friends once, best friends, and that friendship had meant something to Bess. It still stung that it hadn't meant anything at all to Milly.

But Bess had no time for the Unicorn Club tonight. She was here on Odditorium business and still needed to find Professor Ash. She quickly finished her hot frog and made her way to the other stalls. The one she'd thought was selling candyfloss actually sold spiderfloss – white, sparkling and sticky. And the hook-a-duck stand turned out to be hook-a-wereduck. The plastic ducks all had little painted fangs, as well as red-rimmed eyes, and were quite feisty. Every time one of them got hooked, it came to life and started battling against the fishing line with a lot of quacking and growling and a bit of slobbering too.

Suddenly there was a kerfuffle from the other side of the stand. Bess inwardly groaned as she recognised Horace, Milly's brother. He was a couple of years older than her, and he was also a bully and a troublemaker. Even when Bess and Milly had been friends, she'd always dreaded running into Horace. Pops had thrown him out of the Odditorium several times for tormenting Blizzard through the bars or banging on Jessie's cabinet. Pops had believed wholeheartedly in second chances, but Horace had caused so much damage that he'd been permanently banned.

The boy was clearly getting frustrated with his lack of success in hooking a duck. Bess watched him raise his fishing rod and deliberately whack one of the wereducks with it. The duck began honking and shrieking. It thrashed up from the water and bit Horace on the finger before dropping back into the pool with an indignant quack. It was only a little bite, but Horace howled as if half his hand had been chomped off.

"It attacked me! That duck's out of control." He glared at the stallholder. "Where's my prize? I want my prize!"

The woman frowned at him. "There's no prize if you hit the duck rather than hook it. Please leave my stall."

"No way!" Horace threw the fishing rod into the pool with a splash, setting the wereducks off again. "Not until I get my prize."

"She told you to go. There are no prizes for idiots here."

Bess looked round to see the fire-performer girl she'd noticed earlier. She didn't have any fire sticks with her now, but she did have a blazing look of anger in her eyes that any sensible person would have taken heed of.

"I paid to play the game so I deserve a prize," Horace snarled. "You won't get away with this! My dad's the constable of this town. He'll confiscate your ducks and put you all in jail!"

"No, he won't," Bess said.

Horace and Milly's father was indeed the town constable, but Bess knew he was a fair and decent man who despaired of his son's bad behaviour. He'd seemed genuinely regretful when Milly had fallen out with Bess too.

"If your dad found out how you'd behaved just now," she added, "he would be ashamed and make you pick up litter for a week!"

Horace rounded on her, glaring. He was a lot taller than Bess, but she was too cross to feel afraid. The episode had brought to mind all the times Horace had caused trouble in the Odditorium or been rude to her grandfather, not to mention the hurt she still felt over Milly. She stood her ground and returned his glare with a fierce one of her own.

"Bess Harper," he sneered. "The town weirdo. You wouldn't dare tell on me."

"I will!" Bess took a step forward. "Don't forget I know where you live and I know your dad too. He'll believe me if I tell him what you did."

Horace's eyes narrowed and the tips of his ears went red. He hesitated for a moment, but something in Bess's expression must have convinced him she was serious. He threw up his hands and said, "It's rubbish here anyway. I'm going home." He started to stomp off, but then paused beside Bess. "At least now that your grandfather is dead there's one less weirdo in this town," he spat. "Good riddance! See you at school."

Bess felt tears sting her eyes, but she gritted her teeth and blinked them away. A hand tapped her gently on the shoulder and Bess turned to see the fire girl standing next to her.

"Here," she said. "We thought you might like to take the prize."

She was holding out a little teddy bear. It was small enough to fit into the palm of her hand and was clearly a vampire with tiny pointed fangs and a shiny cape.

"Thanks." Bess took the teddy and slipped it into her pocket.

"He won't make things difficult for you at school, will he?" the fire girl asked, looking worried.

Bess shrugged and tried to smile. She knew that Horace wouldn't do anything too bad in front of the teachers, but he was an expert at the kind of sneaky insult and hostile look that could spoil your day. Milly had picked up the same knack from him too.

"School's always difficult," Bess said. "But I don't care about Horace or the others."

"Well, it was nice of you to help," the girl replied. "I should get back for the next performance."

She gave Bess a wave and slipped away into the crowd.

The stallholder was already turning her attention to new customers so Bess left too. She still hadn't seen any sign of Professor Ash and hoped she might come across him inside the train. He had to be there *somewhere* after all. She approached the last carriage in the line where a little queue of people were waiting to go in, including, unfortunately, the Unicorn Club, who all made a big show of ignoring her.

A sign outside promised an abundance of strange marvels and interesting curiosities within, but green velvet drapes hung in all the windows so it was impossible to get a glimpse inside. Bess expected something similar to the Odditorium, with items displayed in cases and cabinets, but she was soon to find out that nothing was kept behind glass in the Train of Dark Wonders.

It seemed that visitors were being let inside in groups, and before long a member of staff said it was time for them to board the train. He was wearing the same green waistcoat as the hot-frog man. He let ten people on altogether, including Bess and the Unicorn Club.

Bess found the light from the wall sconces quite dim compared with the bright torches and flashes of fire outside. The velvet curtains muffled the noise from the fair, making it seem as if all the performers and the stands and the jostling crowds had suddenly gone away. The guests were gathering round something in the middle of the carriage and Bess heard Milly give a squeal of dislike.

It was a horse. Bess thought it was a real one to begin with – it was certainly big enough – but then she realised it was from a carousel. There was a pole going down through its middle, only instead of being garlanded with the usual flowers this one was decorated with tiny bats and blood-red apples.

Bess thought of the poisoned-apple tree tucked into her bag, strangely beautiful just like the horse. The creature shimmered jet black from nose to hoof, with glowing purple berries in its mane and tail. There was no saddle, but Bess supposed this wasn't the type of horse you could ride. It had a wild look in its eyes as if it would throw you straight off if you tried to climb on.

A sign next to it claimed that this was an enchanted fairy-tale horse from a wicked stepmother's carousel and that it could journey through mirrors. A large mirror in an elaborate gold frame stood directly opposite the horse as if inviting people to find out for themselves. Bess was surprised to note that there wasn't any rope keeping the public back. There would be nothing to stop someone from touching the horse, if they were foolish enough.

Bess had been around enough marvels and curiosities to know that you had to respect anything that was even remotely magical, but there was one man in the crowd who obviously hadn't learned that lesson. He was dressed in an orange jacket and his brown hair reached his shoulders and smelled too strongly of oils.

"There's not a chance it's real!" he scoffed. "Just another fake like all that junk in the Odditorium."

Bess bristled. She had half a mind to invite him to inspect Jessie and see how fake he thought the doll was when she stabbed him with a pin. But, before she could say anything, the man was already approaching the horse.

A couple of people suggested that maybe this wasn't a good idea, while everyone else was holding their breath. Bess could tell that they really wanted to see him get on to the horse, just in case something extraordinary happened. She kind of wanted to see it too and watched with rising excitement as the man plonked himself down on the horse's back with a grunt. The horse remained motionless and the crowd let out its breath in a sigh. Bess felt a flash of disappointment. Maybe these things were just impressive fakes after all...

"Told you!" said the man in the orange jacket. "It's not even remotely magical."

But then all of a sudden the horse blinked. Bess saw it and so did several other people in the crowd. It only happened once and you could very easily have missed it, but what you couldn't miss was the fact that the man had vanished from the horse's back. One moment he was there, the next he was gone – but he hadn't gone far.

Milly shrieked and pointed at the mirror. The man was on the other side of the glass, sitting on the reflected carousel horse with a horrified expression on his face. He immediately leaped from the horse's back and ran towards the mirror. His hands pressed against the solid glass and his fingers turned white, but he remained trapped.

"Let me out!" he cried in a panic-filled voice, thumping the glass with his fist. "*Let me out!*"

A female member of staff quickly stepped out of the shadows and told the man to get back on the horse. The moment he climbed up, he vanished from the glass and reappeared in the carriage. He couldn't dismount quickly enough and the other visitors all took a nervous step back. The man was shivering and his teeth were chattering as if it had been very cold inside the mirror.

"A horse from a wicked stepmother's carousel is not to be trifled with," the lady from the train said. "It would bite your hand off sooner than let you pet it and it'll tolerate nothing less than respect. There are further marvels beyond this carriage and they all do exactly what we claim they do. So touch and explore everything by all means, but do not sign up for an experience that you don't truly wish to have."

A hush fell over the crowd as they took this in. Some looked a little uncomfortable, and Milly and her friends left the carriage without looking back. But Bess felt only excitement at the thought of what the rest of the train might hold in store.

Chapter 7

The group entered the second carriage, and Bess expected to see another curiosity, but this time the space was set up for a performance. There were ten chairs, all upholstered in the same emerald velvet she had seen elsewhere. They were arranged in a semi-circle round a pale-skinned boy holding a violin. He looked about eleven or twelve and wore a grey suit that matched the colour of his eyes. His hair was completely white and neatly combed. A little white cat rubbed itself affectionately round his ankles.

Bess took her seat with the other visitors and the boy stepped forward with a shy smile. "My name is Louie Ash," he told them. Bess's ears pricked up. Perhaps he was related to Professor Ash and might be able to tell her where to find him. "And this is my ghost violin," he went on. "It plays graveyard music for the spirit world."

He tucked the instrument beneath his chin and started to play an incredibly eerie tune. Bess couldn't quite work out whether she liked it or not and was still trying to make up her mind when the white cat brushed up against her legs. She leaned down to stroke it, but her fingers passed straight through the animal, which she now saw was faintly transparent. It was a ghost cat!

Bess heard the visitor beside her gasp and looked up to see that more people had come into the carriage. But they were all as transparent as the cat and dressed in old-fashioned clothes. The room was full of ghosts! They applauded enthusiastically when the music finished before fading back to the spirit world. Only the ghost cat remained, trotting over to Louie with its tail held high.

A steward began ushering the visitors from their seats and through to the next carriage, but Bess lingered behind to approach the boy.

"That was amazing," she said.

He gave her a quick smile. "Thank you."

"Are you related to Professor Ash by any chance?"

Louie nodded. "He's my dad."

"Do you think I might be able to speak to him?"

But Louie was already shaking his head. "Dad doesn't leave his office when the train stops. And he never receives visitors without an appointment."

69

The little white cat was brushing round Bess's legs again and she automatically ran her fingers over its ghostly fur. It started to purr as it gazed up at her with bright blue eyes.

"But what if I—" she began.

"Come on, young lady. Time to move on to the next carriage," the train steward interrupted. "Lots of interesting, bewitching things waiting for you in the greenhouse."

"Sorry," Louie said sympathetically. "I'd help if I could, but— Oh! That's funny." He stared down at the white cat then gave Bess a close look.

"What?" Bess asked, wondering whether she had a piece of hot frog stuck between her teeth.

"It's just that Spooky doesn't normally let anyone touch her but me." Louie gestured at the white cat.

"Oh. Maybe she can smell my alligator."

Louie's eyes grew wider. "Your what?"

But, before Bess could reply, the steward had taken her gently by the elbow and was propelling her towards the door. "Got to keep moving through the train, miss," he said cheerfully. "Lots to see."

Bess glanced helplessly back at Louie, who was frowning thoughtfully at the ghost cat. The next moment, the door slid closed behind her and Bess found herself in a carriage with a great number of plant pots. These were no ordinary plants and certainly bore no resemblance to the blooms in Roseville's famous garden. They were even more peculiar than the Odditorium's whispering flowers. For one thing, they each had a large eyeball that swivelled around on a stalk, staring at all the visitors as they passed by. Oozy green sticky stuff dripped from the leaves and their silver petals gave off a peppery scent that made everyone sneeze. Not only that, but it looked as if the plants could move by themselves, scuttling about on their roots in rather a spider-like way.

The fourth carriage held the train's mermaid room, according to a brass plaque on the door. Bess had her own mummified mermaid back at the Odditorium – a grisly, long-dead thing with only a few wisps of hair left on its skeletal head. She expected to find something similar in the train, but to her surprise there were three living mermaids splashing about in an elegant fountain in the middle of the carriage.

Bess edged closer, fascinated, but she made no attempt to touch the mermaids and nor did anyone else in her group. These creatures looked more like something from a nightmare than a fairy tale. About the size of Bess's hand, they had razor-sharp teeth and claws. They snarled at anyone who got too close to the fountain. The sign beside them said that they only sang on the night of a full moon and that their voices alone were enough to kill seabirds, making them fall straight from the sky.

The next carriage contained a purple hedgehog called Bruce who could apparently see the future. And the final one was a dining car serving small cakes in the shape of white cats, along with swampy-looking tea and spider-shaped scones. Dining booths lined the windows and a magnificent castle made from spiderfloss graced the centre of the carriage. A shelf ran all the way round it, up near the ceiling, displaying different kinds of teacups. Inside these were sprawled mischievous little pointy-eared goblins, who kept peering over the side to poke out their tongues and pull faces at the visitors.

Bess longed to take a seat with the others, but there was no time for that. She'd gone all the way through the carriages and still not found Professor Ash or his office. If the show finished and the train left before she could learn where to get the magic beans, then the council might demolish the Odditorium – if the whispering flowers didn't get there first.

She walked down the carriage steps and out into the night, which was full of noise and bright lights. The engine itself was attached to the dining car, puffing smoke out into the dark sky. A red rope was draped across its door, along with a sign saying that visitors weren't allowed in. Bess gazed at it for a moment, wondering if perhaps Professor Ash was inside. But then it occurred to her that while walking through the carriages she hadn't seen a single sleeping compartment or anywhere to store equipment. There'd been no bathrooms or toilets. If all the people who worked here lived on the train, then they must have somewhere to sleep and eat and wash…

She snapped her fingers, feeling triumphant. There had to be more carriages – another part of the train that wasn't here. And now Bess was pretty sure she knew why the Train of Dark Wonders had chosen to stop on Roseville's tallest hill.

ChAPTeR 8

Bess looked down at the forest on the other side of the hill. People rarely went in there because it was full of bats that would swoop down and get tangled up in your hair, so it was the perfect place to hide the rest of the train. The main train track curled round the forest, but perhaps there was a siding somewhere in the trees she didn't know about. She glanced around to make sure no one was watching her and then she quietly slipped away, leaving the hustle and bustle behind as she entered the still darkness of the forest.

Bess didn't mind bats and had been to the forest several times with Pops for a night-time picnic. She started walking, hoping to catch a glimpse of carriages shining through the trees, but it was hard to see much without a torch. The air smelled of moss and damp, and she could hear little creatures scurrying about in the fallen leaves.

Bess had forgotten how large the forest was. The trees all looked the same and before long she wasn't totally sure where she was or which direction she'd come from.

"Bother!" Bess huffed out loud.

She wasn't afraid of the dark and she knew she'd find her way out eventually, but that would take time, and she didn't know how much she might have. The Train of Dark Wonders would need to move out of the way before the mail train came through. She could still hear the fair in the distance, but the trees muffled the sound so it was difficult to judge which direction it came from.

An owl hooted overhead, making her jump. She peered up into the branches, wishing she could speak to the owl and ask it to fly around and help her search. Maybe she was wrong and the other carriages weren't hidden here. Perhaps they'd been left outside town. After all, the gaps between the trees weren't wide enough to accommodate a train siding. Bess felt stupid for thinking that the rest of the train might be here in the first place.

But then a soft little meow came out of the darkness and Bess looked down to see a white cat sitting by her feet. It glowed with a pale light of its own and was slightly transparent. There was no mistaking that this was Louie's ghost cat, Spooky.

"Hello," Bess said. "What are you doing here?"

The cat chirped another meow at her and then took a few steps into the trees before turning back and looking at Bess as if she wanted her to follow.

A grin spread over her face. "Have you come to show me the way to the train?"

The cat continued walking and Bess hurried after her, hope rising in her chest. The route twisted and turned ahead of them, and the sounds of the fair receded. Finally, Bess followed Spooky round the trunk of a particularly large tree and there the missing carriages were in the centre of a clearing. There were twelve of them, all painted black just like the others, their silver stars gleaming in the moonlight.

"Oh!" Bess let out her breath in a delighted gasp. "Thank you, Spooky!"

She couldn't think how the carriages had got here without a track, especially as the ground around them wasn't churned up from their wheels. The carriages were all dark and quiet, with their curtains drawn. Spooky trotted off to the carriage at the end and Bess followed. She wasn't surprised to find that the door was locked. It would have been too easy if it had been open.

Bess had her lock-picking kit with her as always, and could feel the weight of it in her pocket. She started to reach for it, but then hesitated, wondering whether she should knock first. Breaking into the train like a thief wasn't exactly going to create a good first impression. She raised her hand and lightly rapped her knuckles against the door.

"Hello?" she called in a soft voice. "Professor Ash?"

As she'd expected, there was no answer.

She looked down at Spooky, and the ghost cat blinked her blue eyes in an encouraging sort of way. Bess reached into her pocket and selected a pick from the leather pouch. She'd never yet met a lock she couldn't crack – and this one was no different. She heard the lock click in less than two minutes, but at that exact same moment her pick was shoved firmly out of the keyhole by a small object on the other side.

Bess was so surprised that she dropped the pick. She only caught a brief glimpse of the object that had pushed it out, but it looked strangely like… well, like a tiny sword.

Frowning, Bess bent to retrieve her pick. What could possibly have a weapon that small? She thought of the teacup goblins she'd seen back in the dining car and wondered whether one of them was on the other side of the door.

"Hello?" she called. "Who's there? I'd like to speak to Professor Ash, please."

There was no reply, but when Bess pressed her ear to the door she thought she heard a scurrying sound on the other side.

"It's bound to be goblins," she muttered to herself.

Just then she heard the distant whistle of the mail train. It was approaching the hill, which meant she was almost out of time. She reached out to open the door. It swung forward at her touch and golden light spilled out into the darkness. Bess took a deep breath and ventured into the carriage.

Chapter 9

The first thing Bess noticed was that she seemed to be in some kind of kitchen carriage. Everything gleamed silver – there was a sink, a hob and shelves lined with tins of food. A variety of spoons and spatulas hung from a row of hooks on the wall. The second thing she noticed was that she was surrounded by tiny creatures holding swords.

She thought they were goblins at first – they were about the same size – but then she spotted their little round ears, long tails and whiskers and realised they were mice. Not real mice but puppet ones, made from the same felt material as the magician she'd seen back at the rose garden. There was no sign of the boy this time though, or anyone else who might be controlling the puppets. They were dressed in black outfits, including hats and masks with only a narrow gap for their bright, shining eyes to peer through.

Bess gasped in delight. "You're ninja mice!"

The nearest mouse squeaked at her and jabbed its sword emphatically. In fact, all the mice were pointing their swords at her. Through the open door, Bess heard the whistle of the mail train once again and knew she had to act quickly.

"It's okay," she said, holding up her hands. "I'm a friend." An idea suddenly occurred to her and she reached for her backpack. "And I've brought gifts!"

She didn't know whether the mice could understand or not, but their felt ears pricked up at the word "gifts", so she carried on.

"They're in here." She tapped her backpack. "Can I show you?"

She slowly swung her bag down on to the floor, but as soon as she unzipped it the mice all began squeaking loudly and waving their swords.

Bess held her hands up once more. "Why don't you take a look for yourselves?" she suggested. "There are little trunks in there. Go ahead and open them."

The mice looked at each other and carried out a quick squeaking conversation. Then one of them tucked its sword into its belt and performed a series of impressive somersaults and flips across the floor to reach the bag.

Bess couldn't help breaking out into applause. It wasn't every day you saw a puppet ninja mouse doing backflips. The mouse seemed surprised by her reaction, but then stood up a little straighter, preening slightly as it gave a bow. It leaped high into the air in a graceful spinning tuck and landed straight inside Bess's bag. It soon found the dolls' trunks and they came flying out to land in a heap on the floor.

In all her excitement about the train, Bess hadn't got round to inspecting the contents and she could only hope that whatever was stored inside might be of some interest to these mice. One of them stepped forward to examine the nearest trunk. They were just like miniature suitcases, complete with tiny travel stickers, and the mouse deftly released the clasps to open it.

An abundance of dolls' clothes spilled out in a froth of silk sleeves and lace petticoats. Bess felt a flicker of uncertainty. Perhaps tough ninja mice would have no interest in such things. But they let out a flurry of delighted squeaks and immediately rushed forward to grab clothing from the pile.

Bess closed the carriage door and watched as the mice shed their ninja outfits and began wriggling into the dolls' ones. Most of them were ballgowns with tiny buttons at the back. The mice couldn't reach these and they hurried up to Bess, gesturing at her to help, so she knelt on the floor to do up the fastenings.

"You look lovely!" she cried when all the mice had put on their new outfits. "Now I don't suppose you might tell me where Professor Ash is?"

The mice weren't interested in Professor Ash. They were only interested in the suitcases they hadn't opened yet and quickly set to work on the clasps. One contained lavish hats; another was full of towering powdered wigs of the kind that Bess had seen kings and queens wearing in picture books about the olden days. There were gloves, fans and satin-lined capes. Finally, there was only one suitcase left and Bess imagined it would contain ballet slippers or something similar. But, when one of the mice opened it, a collection of little weapons spilled out – jewelled daggers mostly, along with a couple of axes.

"Oh!" Bess exclaimed. "I'm sorry, I didn't realise!"

But the mice were delighted with these most of all.

Bess gave a slight shrug and started to inch past them. Her plan was to head towards the door so she could explore the rest of the train, but she'd only gone a couple of steps when a piercing whistle rang out. She froze, thinking that it didn't sound much like the mail train. Perhaps it was the Train of Dark Wonders? It could be signalling that it was about to depart...

Bess had barely finished the thought when the carriage suddenly lurched as if it were being pulled forward. But how could they be moving when there wasn't an engine attached? And how exactly were the carriages going to get out of the clearing when there were trees crowded all round them?

Bess yanked back the curtains of the nearest window and peered out just in time to see that the train wasn't moving forward at all. It was diving underground!

Chapter 10

It was as if a big hole had suddenly appeared in the forest floor and the train had tipped straight into it. The angle of their descent was so steep that spoons and spatulas fell from their hooks, landing on the floor with a series of clangs. The ninja mice hurried to grab the suitcases before they could slide away and Bess gripped the worktop for support.

She could hear plates and teacups rattling in the cupboards and saw soft, crumbly earth rising up on the other side of the windows. The next moment, the moonlight and the sky and the forest were gone. She could feel that the train was still plummeting, shaking and shuddering as it rattled along some kind of underground tunnel.

The lights flickered in the carriage, but thankfully stayed on. Bess could see absolutely nothing beyond the window except for soil. How would she ever get out? Was she going to be buried alive? She felt a flash of panic that she'd never see her parents or the Odditorium again…

All of a sudden the train levelled out and was travelling straight ahead rather than downwards. Now there were lights glowing on the curved walls. Then the train came to a stop beside a platform. It was almost identical to the one beneath the Odditorium, with its bottle-green bricks, except this one had a sign saying ROSEVILLE STATION. The other difference was that, standing on the platform, there was a huge mole – only a little shorter than Bess herself – dressed in a smart blue suit and a bowler hat.

Bess blinked and shook her head, wondering if she was imagining things. Perhaps she'd fallen and hit her head. Or was she still at home asleep in her bed? Perhaps she'd never gone to the Train of Dark Wonders at all. She scrunched her eyes up tight, but when she opened them again the mole was still there, standing beside a little cart piled high with striped paper bags.

Noticing her looking at him, he held up one of his spade-like paws in a wave. Bess pulled down the carriage window and leaned out.

"Would you like to purchase some refreshments for the journey, miss?" The mole had a croaky voice, a pink nose and chocolate-brown eyes. Bess longed to ask what kind of magical creature he was, or how he could talk, but didn't want to seem rude.

"Um, no, thank you," she said. "But could you tell me where I am?"

The mole looked surprised. "Why, you're in Roseville."

"But…there's no train station like this in Roseville," said Bess.

The mole blinked. "There are underground stations in most towns in the country," he replied. "All over the world in fact. The network of troll tunnels stretches for miles."

Bess could only stare. "Troll tunnels?"

The mole scratched his head, looking puzzled. "Surely you know what troll tunnels are?" He squinted at her. "Does Professor Ash know you're on his train?"

"Oh yes, I'm… I'm doing some work experience," Bess replied, thinking quickly.

The mole didn't look too convinced, but then the hoot of a train whistle echoed down the platform. "Ah, the rest of the train is here," the mole said. "Well, have a good journey, miss."

Before Bess could reply, she heard a clanking noise and the carriage jerked and rocked as the other carriages joined on. Then the engine was travelling forward again. When she craned her head out of the window, she saw the Train of Dark Wonders and the rest of the carriages up ahead. The engine's stars shone in the dimness as it chugged along, billowing steam.

"Enjoy your work experience!" the mole called.

Bess lifted her hand to wave, and the next moment the mole and the platform were gone as the train dived into another tunnel. She turned from the window to see that the ninja mice had vanished, taking the little trunks with them.

Suddenly she heard voices from the next carriage. She froze for a moment, wondering what to do. She knew what she *ought* to do. She should make her presence known straight away and ask to be taken back to Roseville. After all, she wanted to speak to Professor Ash, not actually *leave* with the train. She had no idea where it might be heading or when it would be back. Her parents would be worried sick when they discovered she wasn't in her bed.

And yet…this was a golden opportunity and Bess could feel exhilaration fizzing all the way down to her fingertips. How amazing it would be to travel on the train, to get a taste of a different kind of life, just for a little bit. To go on a real adventure like her pops!

The thought of missing out on all that was unbearable. She then recalled the words Jamie had spoken to her on the steps of the museum:

If you do *happen to find yourself on the train, don't worry about the Odditorium. I can look after the old place while you're gone and keep the flowers in check until you get back…*

It was almost as if he'd known this was going to happen.

Bess didn't want to risk being discovered and thrown off the train before she'd had the chance to speak to the professor, so she looked around for somewhere to hide. The cupboards were full of crockery, food and other supplies. There was no table to duck beneath either. The voices from the next carriage were getting closer and Bess wished desperately that she could somehow turn invisible.

Her time had run out. She could see the handle of the door to the next carriage begin to move downwards. In another moment, someone would come in and she'd be discovered. So Bess did the only thing she could think of – she opened the door she'd entered by a few minutes before and stepped down on to the narrow step outside the carriage. Then she slammed the door closed and held on to the door handle for dear life as the tunnel whistled past her.

Chapter 11

The train seemed to be moving even faster from outside the carriage and Bess wondered whether this was a good idea after all. Her ponytail whipped into her face and her eyes watered. Her plan had been to hide out there until the people in the kitchen moved on, but she felt very exposed with the tunnel walls rushing past her.

Then she spotted a ladder attached to the side of the carriage right next to the door. She grabbed the nearest rung and made her way up to the roof, climbing carefully hand over hand until she reached the top. The tunnel stretched quite high above her so at least she felt as if she had a little more room to breathe up there.

Better still, the train seemed to sense she was there. Perhaps her movement had triggered some mechanism because, all of a sudden, railings slid up from the roof, along with a circular seating area complete with a crackling fire pit. There was even a basket of blankets.

It still felt strange, and a bit hazardous, walking along the roof of the carriage as the train rattled through the tunnel. Bess edged her way to the seats and sat down. From there, she could see all the way along the length of the carriages to the engine at the front. It was quite chilly so she took a blanket from the basket and wrapped it round her shoulders.

Bess had expected the train to continue down the tunnel – and it did for a while – but then it came out into a vast underground cavern. The earth still formed a sort of ceiling above her, dotted here and there with glow-worms, but the walls had fallen away completely.

She stared in amazement as the train rattled past underground forests and streams and even a couple of towns that she guessed belonged to the trolls. There were little circular houses and a lot of bridges, which Bess thought made sense since everyone knew that trolls liked bridges. She wondered if she'd see some Billy Goats Gruff as well, but it was too dark for that. The trolls must have very good night vision without any sunlight to see by. The only source of illumination seemed to be coming from the glow-worms.

Bess stared at it all in wonder for quite some time. Finally, though, her eyes started to ache with tiredness. It was warm and comfortable by the fire and she snuggled down under her blanket, thinking that she'd just close her eyes for a moment or two and then decide what to do next. Unfortunately she must have been more tired that she realised because she soon fell fast asleep.

Bess didn't wake up until a hand gently shook her arm. She opened her eyes, thinking it was her mum come to tell her to get ready for school. Instead, she looked straight up into the face of the boy she'd met on the Odditorium steps. Just like before, his black hair stuck up in all directions, the same as his puppet magician. He was staring at her as if he could hardly believe what he was seeing.

"How did you get here?" he asked. "And – more importantly – how did you get past my ninja mice? They're enchanted to do their job and guard the train whether I'm there or not. They should never have let you in."

Bess blinked, trying to pull her tangle of sleepy thoughts together. When she sat up, she saw that the train had stopped. It looked like they were at another station. And not a small one like Roseville's. This was a much larger affair with a grand vaulted ceiling and a lot of marble pillars. A sign on the wall read DARK CENTRAL STATION in decorative gold tiles. It was hard to tell underground, but Bess guessed it must be early in the morning because there weren't many people about.

The dark-haired boy was still looking at her, waiting for answers to his questions. Since she'd already been discovered, there didn't seem much point in being anything other than honest.

"I gave the mice some dresses," she said. "I guess they were excited by all the colours after only wearing black. Um, I know this looks bad, but I honestly don't mean any harm. I just really need to speak to Professor Ash."

"Well, that's good," the boy said, "because he'll certainly want to speak to you."

"He doesn't know I'm here yet—" Bess started to say.

"He knows," the boy cut in. "Something like this would never get past the professor. And it's not every day someone manages to sneak aboard the Train of Dark Wonders." He peered at her curiously. "The carriages had a cloaking charm on them. You ought to

92

have wandered in the woods for hours without finding them."

"Well, I had some help," Bess replied. "The ghost cat led me there."

The boy looked startled. "Spooky? But she doesn't like outsiders. In fact, she doesn't really like anyone but Louie."

Bess shrugged, not knowing what else to say.

"All right," said the boy. "Well, follow me. I'll take you to the professor. My name's Beau, by the way."

"I'm Bess."

She scrambled to her feet, placed the blanket neatly back in the basket and went after Beau. Instead of going down the nearest ladder, he walked along the top of the carriages and didn't stop until he was right at the front, at the engine itself. Bess followed him down the ladder to the small platform outside the door. The red rope and sign about visitors had been removed. Beau knocked once and a man's voice called for them to come in.

They opened the door and Bess entered, expecting to see a driving compartment of some kind, but the space inside was more like a study or a library. There were books everywhere, lining the shelves and stuffed into every corner, even piled up in unsteady towers upon the floor.

A long metal bar was attached to the ceiling and from this a large creature dangled upside down. It looked like a massive bat, with leathery wings curled round itself. It was completely motionless and Bess couldn't tell if it was real or not. A big desk took up one corner and there was a little fireplace directly beneath the train's funnel. A fire crackled in the grate, and in the armchair before this sat a man.

Even seated, Bess could tell that he was tall and quite thin. He was dressed in a green waistcoat over a white shirt, striped trousers and polished brown shoes. His nose was bent at the bridge and he wore a wiry pair of glasses. One long leg was crossed over the other and Bess saw that he was wearing odd socks. His chestnut-brown hair was flecked with grey above his ears and he was holding a book, but he put this down as the children walked in.

"Morning, professor," Beau greeted him. "I'm guessing you already know about our visitor?"

"Yes, indeed." Professor Ash stood up and walked over to Bess, gazing down at her with kind, curious brown eyes. "Mish informed me that there was a girl sleeping on the roof. Most puzzling. I always prefer a warm, comfortable bed myself. But where are my manners? How do you do? I'm Professor Barnaby Ash."

He offered Bess his hand to shake as if she were a grown-up. She took it and said, "I know who you are, sir. I wanted to speak to you at Roseville, but everyone said you don't appear at the shows."

"That's correct," the professor said pleasantly. "I don't leave the train while the performances are going on."

"But why?"

Bess was confused. If the Odditorium ever ended up full of visitors, she could imagine nothing she'd like more than mingling with them, answering questions about the curiosities and accepting compliments from the guests.

"I mean…this is your train, isn't it?" she asked.

Professor Ash tilted his head slightly to one side. "Well, yes. In a sense," he said. "The carriages and the

95

locomotive belong to me, if that's what you mean. But as for the people and marvels that travel with us, they belong to no one but themselves. I prefer not to be present for the shows because I am a shy man and large crowds of people make me quite nervous, especially if they're all wanting to talk to me, expecting me to say clever and amusing things. However, it is not an easy task to sneak aboard the Train of Dark Wonders so I can only imagine that you wanted to discuss something important?"

"Oh yes, it's very important," Bess replied, relieved that the professor seemed willing to listen and wasn't about to throw her off his train.

"In that case," Professor Ash said, "I will ring for a fresh pot of tea, and you'd best take a seat and tell me all about it."

Chapter 12

Professor Ash poured tea for himself, Bess and Beau. It was an inky midnight blue colour and tasted faintly of sherbet. Bess liked the way it fizzed on her tongue.

She set her cup down carefully and then launched into her story. When she mentioned how her grandfather had recently died, she was surprised to see tears gleaming in the professor's eyes.

"I am truly sorry to hear this news," he said. "Henry was… He was my dear friend and one of the best men I've known. When he didn't come to find me at the show last night, I hoped he'd got caught up in some important business."

"You were expecting to see him there?"

"Of course. Why would he use the ticket to call the train if he didn't intend to visit?"

Bess thought of the golden ticket she'd fed into the machine on the underground platform. "The ticket brought you to Roseville?"

Professor Ash nodded. "He always used it to let me know he wanted to see me. Usually we go to the station below the Odditorium, but since we haven't put on a show in your town for many years, I thought we'd stop on the hill."

"How did you know Pops?" Bess asked. "He never mentioned the train."

"Ah, well, he couldn't talk about it in any detail. We swear all visitors to secrecy, you see, so that they can't share any of our secrets. Your grandfather and I met through the train actually. In fact, we went on an adventure or two together in our time. He travelled with us occasionally, looking for artefacts for his museum. You must miss him dreadfully."

Bess felt a lump rise in her throat. She nodded. "I do. Every day. Sometimes I can hardly believe that I'll never see him again. It doesn't feel real. But at least I still have the Odditorium. I guess you must have been there? We have these whispering flowers, and Pops left a note saying they need magic beans to survive, but we've run out and he said you'd be happy to assist. I really need your help because the flowers are so hungry they've started breaking into the museum, looking for food. My uncle says it's a safety hazard and he's reported us to the council. And the building will be demolished at the end of the month if I don't find food for the flowers."

She finished her sentence in a bit of a rush and held her breath, waiting. Professor Ash had been listening intently the entire time, with the tips of his fingers resting lightly together. Now he leaned forward slightly.

"My dear, I am familiar with Harper's Odditorium of course. I've been there many times to catch up with your grandfather and inspect the curiosities. There are some fine collections there and I know all about the whispering flowers. Normally I'd be more than happy to help you track down some magic beans, but the train is on a mission that can't wait. We're on our way to the Land of Halloween Sweets to seek out a ghostly gobstopper. Have you heard of those? Extremely rare. Extremely interesting. It's vital we find one and the door to the land will only stay open for a short while."

Bess was quite thrilled by the mention of doors to other lands, but the professor went on before she could ask any questions.

"We can't afford to delay, I'm afraid. Perhaps we might be able to help you once we return? Our mission will take no more than a few days. It will be simple enough to arrange for another train to take you back to the platform beneath the Odditorium."

Bess felt deflated. It didn't seem fair that she should have come all this way only to leave empty-handed. What if the train didn't come back? Or what if their mission took longer than expected? She felt strongly that if she left the train now she wouldn't see it again in time to save the museum. Her mind raced as an idea began to form.

"Can I come with you?" she asked. "Pops said in his letter that the whispering flowers need magical food – it doesn't have to be beans as long as they can chew it. Perhaps I might be able to buy something in the Land of Halloween Sweets."

Professor Ash paused. Bess could sense Beau watching them as he sipped his tea.

"This train doesn't normally take on passengers," the professor said apologetically. "It's a working train, you see, full of peculiar things as I'm sure you're already aware. It's not really set up for people who don't know their way around. Why, you might wander into the wrong compartment and be eaten alive by one of the exhibits."

Bess couldn't tell if he was joking or not. "I'd be very careful," she promised. "And only go into the places where I was allowed. I know all about being vigilant from the museum."

She hurried to tell him about Blizzard and how fond she was of the alligator.

"Ah, yes, a most noble creature from what I recall," the professor said. "I can well imagine that you'd be fond of him. I feel the same way about Pickwick over there." He gestured at the bat hanging from the metal bar.

"Is he real then?" Bess asked.

"Indeed. He's a flying fox. Otherwise known as a fruit bat."

The bat had been as still as a statue, but now, as if sensing he was being spoken about, he unfurled one of his wings and poked his head out to peer at Bess. He did look curiously like a fox with his long ears and pointed snout. Bess could tell he was old because his muzzle was grey.

"I adore bats," Professor Ash went on. "Pickwick has been my companion for many years."

"Then you understand how I feel about Blizzard," Bess said. "I have a responsibility to him as well as the other exhibits. It would break my heart if the Odditorium was demolished. It's my grandfather's legacy. Please let me come with you."

"I'm not unsympathetic to your difficulties, my dear," the professor said gently. "It would indeed be a great pity if Henry's Odditorium were no more." He rubbed at his chin for a moment. Finally, he sighed and said, "Since you're Henry's granddaughter, perhaps I might make an exception. You will have to ask your parents whether they agree though. I won't take you anywhere without their consent."

Bess frowned. "But…how am I supposed to ask them? Will another train take me back to Roseville?"

Professor Ash shook his head. "Oh no, there's no time for that," he said. "The door to the land we're travelling to will only be open for a short while. But there is a mirror in your home somewhere, I presume?"

"Yes, several of them. But why does that matter?"

"If there's a mirror, then you can use Echo to speak to your parents."

"Echo?" Bess repeated, confused.

"The carousel horse," Professor Ash explained. "I expect you saw her at the show?"

"Oh. Yes, I did. I thought she was wonderful."

"If you're brave enough to climb on her back," the professor said, "then she can take you to the mirror inside your house."

ChapTer 13

Professor Ash opened the door of the locomotive and ushered Bess out on to the platform. Beau seemed like he wanted to come with them, but the professor turned to him and said, "You have puppet matters to deal with, I imagine?"

"Yes, professor," Beau said, looking more than a little disappointed. He glanced at Bess and gave her a wave. "Good luck with your parents. I hope they let you come with us."

Bess smiled, pleased as well as surprised that he cared one way or the other. His words gave her a warm feeling in her tummy and she hoped more fiercely than ever that her parents might understand.

She followed Professor Ash down the platform. It seemed livelier now than it had before. There were porters in smart red uniforms trimmed with gold braid helping people with their luggage. At least *some* of the travellers on the platform were people, even if they were dressed in weird and wonderful-looking outfits. Others didn't seem to be human at all.

Bess saw a human-sized orange cat with elegant whiskers wearing a green suit and top hat strolling along the platform. And a penguin in an opera cape, carrying a silver-topped cane under one wing and a rolled-up newspaper in the other, was honking orders at a valet in a bossy sort of way. There was a plant scuttling about on its roots, shedding a trail of pink blossoms behind it, and even a skeleton wearing a top hat sitting on a bench. It was attempting to eat a croissant, but the pastry just fluttered through its ribs and landed in a sad pile on the floor – a sight that the skeleton took in with much sighing.

Even the other trains seemed out of the ordinary. The one on the platform opposite the Train of Dark Wonders had green and purple fur and lots of little legs. It actually looked more like a gigantic caterpillar than a train. And the one beyond that was a bright candy pink and blew bubbles from its funnel instead of steam. Bess longed to stop and take it all in, but Professor Ash was striding ahead and she had to hurry to keep up.

"What *is* this place?" she asked, gazing around in wonder.

"This? Why, this is Dark Central Station – the largest station in the entire Troll Network," Professor Ash replied. "All lines pass through here at some point."

"The Troll Network?" Bess asked.

"A network of tunnels dug by trolls many thousands of years ago," the professor explained. "Some of them are simply a fast and convenient way of travelling from A to B. There are numerous short cuts, you see. For example, one of the lines will get you from London to Shanghai in a little over two hours, which is considerably faster than flying. But it's the purple-line tunnels that are of most interest to us. They lead to other worlds. Quite fascinating. Ah, here we are."

He stopped in front of one of the carriages, sprang up the steps and opened the door. A massive tentacle flopped out, almost knocking the professor off his feet. It was a vivid blue colour – the brightest blue Bess had ever laid eyes on – and it began to thrash about energetically, feeling along the ground as if looking for something. Bess leaped back, alarmed. Whatever was inside this carriage must be some fearsome beast, easily big enough to gobble up a person alive.

"Oh fiddlesticks!" the professor exclaimed. He dived beneath one of the tentacles and snatched something from the steps. When he held it up, Bess saw it was a teddy bear and guessed it must have tumbled out when the door opened. "Apologies, madam," Professor Ash said. "So terribly rude of me." He pressed the bear into the flailing tentacle, which curled round it tightly and withdrew into the carriage in a huffy sort of way.

Professor Ash slammed the door closed and shook his head. "How foolish! Of course, that's Barbara's carriage now." He glanced back at Bess. "I forgot that they moved everything around after the eyeballs incident."

"The eyeballs incident?" Bess repeated. "What kind of animal is Barbara?"

"Oh, Barbara is... Well, she's..." Professor Ash trailed off as if not quite sure how to answer the question. Then he shook his head. "It's a little hard to explain about Barbara actually. All in good time. Come along. Echo's carriage is the next one over. At least I'm seventy-eight percent certain that it's this one."

They went to the next carriage and Professor Ash poked his head inside first before saying, "Yes, this is it."

He beckoned Bess forward and she stepped inside, expecting the carriage to look like the one where she'd seen the carousel horse before. But this carriage appeared to be some sort of stable. A narrow walkway led down one side and on the other there was a row of stalls. Bess could just about see over the top of the doors and that was when she realised that these were no ordinary horses. The first stall held a zebra with green and black stripes. The second had a two-headed donkey. The third appeared to be empty at first, but then Bess heard a snorting huff of breath and saw the sign on the door that read STALL CONTAINS INVISIBLE HORSE. DO NOT USE FOR STORAGE.

The fourth stall housed Echo, along with several mirrors. Professor Ash unbolted the door and opened it wide for Bess. "She's all yours," he said. "Just put this on first." He reached up to a hook on the wall and brought down a velvet-lined cloak. "It's very cold inside a mirror," he said. "You won't want to be there any longer than you have to so try to explain things to your parents as quickly as you can. We wouldn't want frostbite to set in."

Again, Bess wasn't quite sure whether or not he was joking, but she remembered how the man at the show had shivered after being in the mirror for only a few seconds. She took the cloak and threw it over her shoulders.

"How do I get to the mirror in my parents' house?" she asked.

"Just tell Echo where you want to go," the professor replied. "And then hold on tight."

Bess approached the carousel horse, feeling a mixture of nervousness and excitement. She longed to give Echo a pat, but she remembered what the steward had said before about the horse biting. "Hello," she said quietly. "Could you please take me to— Oh!"

She broke off in surprise as the carousel horse walked forward and thrust her head into her arms with a whinny of pleasure. When Bess glanced over at Professor Ash, she saw an odd expression on his face. He didn't seem surprised exactly, but he had the wondering look of someone witnessing something they'd never seen before.

Echo obviously didn't usually show much affection, but perhaps she could sense how much Bess liked strange things. That was the only possible explanation. Bess patted the horse gently on her dark neck, then reached up on her tiptoes to whisper in her ear. "Please take me to the mirror in my living room."

Bess wasn't sure where in the house her parents might be, but there wasn't a mirror in the kitchen and she didn't want to pop up and startle anyone when they were in the bathroom so the living room seemed like the best bet.

She walked round to pull herself up on to Echo's back. She'd only just sat down when Professor Ash said, "Oh, I almost forgot. Take this for when your parents ask about school."

"School?"

Bess had been so fixed on whether her parents would allow her to go with the train that she hadn't even considered the problem of school. Before she could ask any questions, the professor tossed her a little package. Then the carriage around her vanished and she found herself on the other side of the mirror.

CHAPTER 14

B ess was very glad of the cloak. It was icy cold inside the mirror and she was surrounded by ribbons of frosty mist. Straight ahead she could see Professor Ash standing on the other side of a mirror in Echo's stall. He raised his hand in a brief wave, gave her an encouraging smile, then disappeared. The mirror rippled and the image was replaced with her living room. Bess could see the rose-patterned sofas, the half-finished jigsaw puzzle on the coffee table and the framed paintings of flowers on the walls.

There was no sign of her mum or dad though and Bess felt a flash of dismay. She hadn't thought through what might happen if they weren't there. They could be upstairs or out of the house altogether – perhaps down at the police station reporting her missing. Bess's fingers were already turning blue and she knew she wouldn't be able to stay inside the mirror for long.

Still clutching the package Professor Ash had given her, she hopped down from the horse and hurried over to the mirror. She rapped sharply on it with her knuckles and called through the glass. "Mum? Dad? Hello – is anyone there?"

To her relief, she heard the clatter of feet and then her parents rushed into the room. They looked frazzled, but their faces lit up at the sight of her and Bess felt horribly guilty for any worry she'd caused.

"There you are!" her dad exclaimed. "I thought you'd turn up in a mirror eventually. So you're on the train then?"

"Yes, but…h-how did you know?" Bess stammered.

"Where else would you possibly be?" Mr Harper sighed. "I grew up with your grandfather, remember. I know all about the Train of Dark Wonders and Professor Ash."

"You do?" Bess frowned. "But I thought—"

"Bess, you should never have sneaked off like that," her mum interrupted, looking tearful. "We were so worried."

"I know. And I really am sorry. But I just… I thought the train might help me find a way to save the Odditorium."

As quickly as she could, Bess told her parents about everything that had happened. "And Professor Ash says I can stay on the train for a few days, if you agree," she finished.

She held her breath, waiting for their response, her heart pounding. It seemed impossible that they would be okay with any of this. Her parents would never be able to understand why she wanted to go. It all felt quite hopeless...

But then her mum surprised her by saying, "Yes, Bess. Your father and I have already talked about it and you can go. Just this once."

Bess could hardly believe her ears. "I *can*?"

"Yes," her dad said. "Professor Ash gave you a scarecrow, I suppose?"

"A what?"

"A scarecrow," he repeated. "For school."

Remembering the professor's package, Bess quickly unwrapped it. There was a little scarecrow inside. He was made of straw, with buttons for eyes, and wore a shabby blue coat and a floppy hat.

Bess stared at it. "How is this going to help with school?"

"The scarecrow will go in your place," her dad explained. "It will hang its coat up on your peg, sit at your desk, do your homework and so on. That way no one will notice that you're gone."

Bess shook her head. "I think Miss Benn will notice if there's a scarecrow sitting at my desk."

"It's enchanted," Mr Harper said. "Everyone who looks at it on school grounds will only see you."

"Oh." Bess smiled, delighted. "Wait, how do you know about the scarecrow and what it can do?"

"Because I travelled on the train once myself."

Bess could hardly believe it. "*You?* On the Train of Dark Wonders?"

Her father gave a small smile. "I was young once too, Bess. I know what it feels like to get swept up in ideas of adventure. I thought I wanted to go on one myself, but...well, everyone thinks that when they're eleven years old. You should bear in mind that a real adventure is different from one that's make-believe. You might find that there's more hardship and less fun than you'd imagined. And then perhaps you'll realise that it's rather nice being at home, living a normal, safe, comfortable life. One adventure was enough for me. Perhaps it will be the same for you too."

Bess could see the hope in her parents' eyes and she realised this was why they'd agreed. They believed that it might cure her thirst for adventure and afterwards

113

she'd be content to settle down for good. Maybe they were right, but Bess didn't think so. Pops had never lost *his* thirst for adventure after all. Each one he went on left him wanting more and more, and Bess was sure she'd feel the same way. But if this was the reason her parents were letting her go, then she wasn't going to argue.

"Thank you," she said instead. "Thank you so much."

Bess remembered how the man at the show hadn't been able to pass through the mirror. She looked down at the scarecrow and said, "How do I give it to you?"

"It can travel through the glass," her dad told her. "Just throw it over."

Bess did as he'd said and watched the scarecrow sail into her living room. Her dad caught it and put it carefully into his pocket.

Mrs Harper walked up to the mirror and laid her hand flat against the glass. "Promise you'll be careful, Bess," she said, blinking back tears.

"I promise," Bess said at once.

She put her own hand on the mirror, lining it up with her mum's as if they were touching each other through the glass. Bess could feel only the cold mirror under her skin, but inside her head she felt the warmth of her mother's palm. It made her think of being cuddled on the sofa and tucked into bed each night and kissed on the top of her head. Safe and loved.

All of a sudden she felt a wave of uncertainty. Was she doing the right thing? Should she just go back home – was that where she truly belonged? But sometimes you had to take a risk to get something you really wanted. Bess knew she would never save the Odditorium if she stayed.

It was so cold inthe mirror that she was shivering, so she thanked her parents again and waved her hand. "Goodbye for now," she said. "I promise I'll see you soon."

Mrs Harper stepped back and Mr Harper put his arm round her. Bess knew how difficult it was for them to let her go, and she felt a great surge of love and gratitude towards them both.

"We love you," her dad said.

"Keep safe," her mum added.

"I will," Bess promised. "And I love you too."

She walked back to Echo and reached up to whisper in the horse's ear. "Please take me back to the Train of Dark Wonders."

Bess swung herself up on to the horse's back. She gave her parents one last smile, willing them to know that it would all be okay. Then the image inside the mirror rippled once more. The next moment, her parents had vanished and Bess found herself back in the stable carriage with Professor Ash waiting by the door.

"How did it go?" he asked.

"They said yes!" Bess beamed, scrambling down from Echo's back and handing over the cloak.

"Excellent." The professor rubbed his hands together. "In that case, Miss Harper, we have an adventure to prepare for."

ChAPTER 15

"Under normal circumstances I would offer you a tour of the train and formally introduce you to everyone, but there's no time for that now," Professor Ash said. "I have matters to attend to for our journey so I shall entrust you to Beau's care."

Bess and the professor were standing on the platform. She looked around, but there was no sign of Beau anywhere.

"Mish will take you to him," Professor Ash added.

Bess remembered the professor mentioning this name earlier and wondered who it might be. She expected a person to appear from somewhere, but instead Professor Ash rummaged in the pockets of his waistcoat.

"Now where has he got to?" he muttered.

Bess stared as the professor proceeded to pull out a variety of items: a bright gold feather, a rubber duck, a tiny cactus in a glass bubble and a striped umbrella that was far too big to have fitted into a little pocket in the first place.

"How did you get all that in there?" Bess asked, still staring.

"Hmm?" Professor Ash glanced at her. "Oh, it's... Penelope makes all my clothes, you see. Most convenient."

Bess didn't see at all, but before she could enquire further the professor opened up the umbrella. The canopy sprang open and a large speckled butterfly fluttered out from between the folds, closely followed by a little frog, which leaped on to Professor Ash's shoulder in a single bound.

"Oh fiddlesticks, I was sure Mish was in here somewhere!" the professor exclaimed. "Perhaps he went off to have breakfast or partake in the— Ah! *Here* he is, the rascal!"

He drew his hand out from one of the pockets and attached to his finger was the smallest bat Bess had ever laid eyes on. It was covered in soft black fur and was barely bigger than the professor's thumb.

"This is Mish," Professor Ash said. "He can be a mischievous fellow but is good-natured enough really."

"He's teensy!" Bess gasped.

"Indeed, yes. He's a bumblebee bat. The smallest type in the world. Unfortunately he lost his home when the caves he lived in were taken over as a tourist attraction. He'll show you the way to Beau. Oh, and I almost forgot."

Professor Ash reached into his waistcoat one last time and brought out a ticket. It was like the one Pops had left for Bess back at the museum, only it was mostly black and edged in gold.

"Take this. It's a guest pass for the train. I'd keep it with you at all times. It will let everyone know you have permission to be here and that you aren't an intruder. Some of our company can be a little…well, a bit unforgiving to intruders and we wouldn't want any unfortunate misunderstandings."

Bess took the ticket and tucked it into her pocket.

"I'll have to swear you to secrecy about the train too, I'm afraid," the professor said. "We do this for all visitors, your grandfather included. It would be much harder to operate if too many people knew about us."

"Of course," Bess said. "I won't say a word."

"Might I trouble you to swear upon the rubber duck?" Professor Ash said. He drew the duck back out of his pocket. Bess was puzzled, but did as he'd asked, laying her fingers lightly on the duck's head as she made the promise. The next moment, Mish unfurled his tiny wings and fluttered off towards the train.

"Quick now," Professor Ash urged, stuffing the duck back in his pocket. "The train will be leaving any minute." He flashed her a smile. "And welcome aboard, Miss Harper."

Bess grinned back, then turned and hurried off after the little bat. He flittered and fluttered along the platform in a zigzag motion before swooping through the open window of a carriage. At the same moment, the train gave a piercing whistle and a mole platform attendant announced that it was time to board.

Bess jumped up on to the steps just in time. Smoke billowed down the platform as the train pulled away. Still grinning, she opened the carriage door with tingling fingers and went inside. A brass plaque attached to the wall read CARRIAGE 3544, SLEEPER CARRIAGE. DANGER LEVEL: GREEN.

Bess stared. *Danger level?* She could only hope that green meant it wasn't too perilous. Mish bobbed in the air ahead, waiting for her, so she stepped forward and followed him down the carriage. With its narrow corridor, it was rather like the stable carriage she'd visited earlier, except this one had compartments instead of stalls. The windows were frosted so she couldn't see inside, but she guessed this was where the train staff slept.

Through the corridor windows she saw that the train had left the station, then everything went dark as they entered a tunnel. It took Bess's eyes a moment to adjust to the flickering glow of the orange lamps mounted on the walls. As the train picked up speed, it became harder to walk in a straight line and she had to concentrate on keeping her balance as she followed Mish. The little bat flew past several compartments before finally stopping at the one at the end of the corridor. He glanced back to make sure Bess had seen him, his dark eyes gleaming in the dimness, and then swooped to the ground. He was so tiny that he was able to wriggle right underneath the closed door.

Bess hesitated, wondering what to do. Would Mish be able to tell Beau she was here? She waited a moment, but no one came out and she couldn't hear anything above the *clackety-clack* of the wheels on the track. She lifted her hand and knocked on the door.

"Um...hello?" she called.

The door opened an instant later and Beau peered out. "Aha!" He gave her a big smile. "So you're staying with us after all. Excellent! Come in. You're just in time to join us for breakfast."

Chapter 16

Bess stepped into the compartment, closing the door behind her. She found herself in a tiny – but perfectly designed – bedroom. A bunk bed took up the wall beside the door. Opposite there was just about space for a small armchair and a table with a fringed lamp and a breakfast tray set upon it. The plates and teacups were all emblazoned with a little black train and the ornate initials DW, which Bess guessed stood for Dark Wonders. Steam curled from the spout of a handsome silver teapot and there was a plate piled high with breakfast pastries. The wallpaper was dark green and stamped with lines of silver train tracks.

But Bess was most interested in the carriage's occupants. As before, Beau was dressed all in black. Louie was there too, sitting on the top bunk with his legs dangling over the side. He no longer wore the suit she'd seen him in the day before, but a dark green dressing gown bearing the same insignia as the plates and cups.

The two boys obviously shared this compartment. Bess could see a black violin mounted on the wall above the top bunk, along with a neatly stacked row of books on a shelf. There was another shelf attached to the wall beside the bottom bunk on which sat several puppets, all made from felt: a thief, a jester, a vampire, a cowgirl and a pirate, complete with his own small green parrot.

"Hello again," Louie said, smiling down at her. "I'm glad you managed to speak to my father in the end. It seemed like it was quite important."

"Thanks," Bess said. "It was. He was really helpful."

"Would you like a croissant?" Beau asked. "There isn't any jam, I'm afraid, because Mish is swimming in it. He *always* heads straight for the jam for some reason. Anything sticky really and Mish will be there in the middle of it all, making a mess."

Bess saw that the tiny bat had indeed flown straight into the jam bowl and was rolling about in delight, making excited squeaks.

"There's plenty of butter though," Louie said, hopping down from the bunk.

"And if you *really* want jam then we could always try to get some off Mish?" Beau said. "I'm sure I've a scraper around here somewhere. It'll only taste a little bit like bat."

"Oh, that's okay," Bess replied. "Butter is good."

Louie cut open a croissant and buttered it for her, handing it over with a shy smile. Because of his white hair, he looked quite different from Professor Ash at first glance, but Bess could still see a resemblance. They both had the same quiet, kind eyes and reserved manner. Louie invited Bess to take the armchair.

Meanwhile, Beau offered to stow her backpack in one of the luggage compartments. When she handed it over, he gasped and said, "What's in this thing? Are you carrying bricks? It weighs a ton!"

"It's my poisoned-apple tree," Bess replied.

"Your what?"

"Here, I'll show you."

Bess reached for the bag and pulled out the book. As she opened it, the miniature apple tree unfolded from the pages. Bess was pleased to see it was looking a little better. The leaves weren't drooping quite so much and there was even a bit of blossom on one of the branches.

"Fascinating!" Louie exclaimed when Bess told them what it was.

"It really is!" Bess said. "One time there were all these tiny lanterns hanging from the branches. Another day all the apples turned completely white."

Bess left the tree on the table while they ate their croissants. The two boys sat on the bottom bunk opposite her.

"Oh hello, Spooky," Bess said as the ghost cat jumped down from the top bunk to rub round her ankles. After a moment, the cat hopped up on to her lap, purring contentedly.

"I understand why Spooky likes you now," Louie said. "She used to be your grandfather's cat. When she was alive, I mean."

Bess looked down at the white cat. Now that Louie mentioned it, she *did* recall seeing a white cat in some of Pops's old photos.

"That must be why she helped me find the train."

"How did you manage to get through the door anyway?" Beau asked. "My mice say they didn't let you in so unless they're fibbing to get out of trouble—"

"They're not fibbing," Bess said. "I picked the lock."

Beau looked impressed. "Well, you must be very skilled," he said. "Even Pedro over there can't pick the train's locks." He gestured to his puppet thief lolling at an angle on the shelf.

"Pops always said I was born to be a jewel thief," Bess replied. "Oh, not that I'm going to steal anything of course," she added quickly. "I'm just trying to find a way to save the Odditorium."

"Beau told me all about it," Louie said. "It sounds wonderful. And you're bound to find something for your whispering flowers to eat in the Land of Halloween Sweets."

He got up to pour cups of tea and handed one to Bess. This time the tea was green and tasted of peppermint.

"The door to this particular land only opens once about every hundred years," Beau said. He glanced at Louie then went on, "It's a unique opportunity. We've all been waiting for this for a very long time."

"Here, let me show you the almanac entry," Louie said.

He put aside his empty teacup then climbed the ladder to the bookshelf above his bed. He pulled out a leather-bound volume and jumped back down to hand it to Bess.

She gazed at the front cover. Golden letters stamped out its title – *The Troll Network Almanac*. Inside was information about dozens of different magical lands, including details as to when and how they could be reached via the underground train network. As she leafed through the pages, Bess couldn't help thinking it was just the right size for pressing a tree and wondered what kind of specimen it would produce.

"I've bookmarked the Land of Halloween Sweets," Louie said.

Bess flicked to the marked page and scanned her eyes down the entry. It seemed that there were all kinds of magical sweets in this world and her heart soared at the thought of being able to bring some of them home with her. She saw that there were various maps of the land included in the book as well.

"We don't know how useful those will be," Beau said, peering over her shoulder. "This information was put together a hundred years ago when the door was last open. Things might have changed since then. But hopefully not too much. It looks like we'll only have three days and two nights there before the door closes. If we don't want to get trapped in the land, then we'll have to be out before sunset on the third day."

"It sounds like there are loads of amazing things to see," Bess said. "So, even if you don't find the gobstopper, you could always bring back something else instead."

Beau shook his head. "It has to be the gobstopper." He suddenly looked very serious. "We're not leaving without it."

Something in his tone made Bess pause. "Why? What's so special about it?"

Louie cleared his throat in a pointed sort of way and Beau shook his head. "It's just a very rare sweet, that's all. And the Train of Dark Wonders is all about rare things. Now how about a tour? I can explain how living on the train works and show you where you're going to sleep."

Bess was still curious about the ghostly gobstopper. She sensed there was more to it than Beau was telling her, but it looked like she'd have to let it go for now.

"Sounds great," she said. "I'd love to see the rest of the train."

She handed the almanac back and then reached for her poisoned-apple tree, gently folding it away within the pages of the book.

"We'll leave Louie to what he's best at," Beau said, "which is lounging about in his dressing gown, thinking deep thoughts and playing the violin."

Louie rolled his eyes, but Bess could tell he didn't really mind.

"What does the black violin do?" she asked.

"Pardon?" Louie said, although Bess was fairly certain he'd heard her.

"The black violin," she said again, pointing at the instrument mounted beside his bunk. "If the white one summons ghosts, then what does the black one do?"

"Oh." Louie and Beau exchanged a glance. "It... does something else," Louie finally said. "Um...it exorcises ghosts. I don't like it very much. I'd rather play music for ghosts than banish them to the spirit world. I've only ever played it a couple of times. For troublesome poltergeists."

"There are far more interesting things on the train than Louie's violins," Beau said. "We should just about have time for a tour before we arrive at the gate. If we get a move on."

Bess took the hint. She slung her backpack over her shoulder and gave Louie a wave before following Beau out into the corridor as the train rattled on through the darkness.

CHAPTER 17

"Right," Beau said, rolling up his sleeves. "So the first thing you need to know about is the danger levels." He pointed to a brass plaque on the wall, identical to the one Bess had noticed at the end of the sleeper carriage. "Every carriage has one of these. The plaque provides the carriage number and name, as well as the danger level. And that's the important bit. Green means it's probably safe. Amber means go carefully. And red means it's extremely perilous and you shouldn't go in no matter what. Understand?"

Bess nodded. "How many red carriages are there?"

Beau lifted his shoulders in a shrug. "Sometimes it's none at all. Other times it's three or four. It depends who and what is travelling with the train. Things move around here. At the moment, the train has eighteen carriages and I think only two of them are red."

"Does that include Barbara's carriage?" Bess asked, thinking of the giant blue tentacle she'd seen earlier.

"Definitely," Beau said.

Before Bess could ask what Barbara was exactly, Beau was already opening the door to the little platform joining the carriages.

"The plaques are on the doors too – look. We're right outside Barbara's carriage now in fact." He pointed at the door up ahead, which was fastened with a brass plaque reading CARRIAGE 2711, MENAGERIE CARRIAGE. DANGER LEVEL: RED.

"If you need to get past a red carriage, then you should go up on to the roof." Beau pointed at the carriage wall and Bess saw that there was a ladder attached.

Beau scrambled up it and Bess hurried after him. She found herself on top of the train once again. The train was chugging through the tunnel at a brisk rate, blowing Bess's ponytail back as she made her way across the roof. They climbed back down the ladder at the other end of the carriage and Beau resumed his whistle-stop tour of the train. Along with the carriages she'd already seen, there were various storage cars for the exhibits, a bar, a library, a saloon, an observation carriage, several bathrooms and a bat roost filled with bats and moths – all marked danger level green.

"And this is the wardrobe where Penelope makes the clothes," Beau said, opening another door.

It was filled with racks and racks of garments and accessories bursting with colour. There were feathers and sequins and silks and scarves. Fantastic hats were lined up on a shelf. There were also trunks overflowing with gloves, belts and shoes. A full-length mirror stood in one corner beside a towering pile of striped hatboxes. Bess remembered what Professor Ash had said about Penelope making his waistcoat and realised she must be a very talented seamstress.

"These things are beautiful," she said, staring at a pair of sparkly emerald slippers.

"Beautiful?" Beau looked surprised as if he hadn't considered this. "I suppose so, but they're a lot more than that. They're magic. Penelope can sew a jacket pocket big enough to fit an elephant inside. Or a cloak that will make you invisible. Or shoes that let you run at a hundred miles an hour. Don't even get me started on what the gloves and hats can do. Shall I introduce you?"

Bess was puzzled. "But…I can't see anyone."

Beau grinned. "She's still sleeping probably. Penny likes a lie-in. It's about time she was up though."

He walked over to the tower of hatboxes and rapped his knuckles gently against the side of the one on top.

"Rise and shine, Penny!" he called.

There was a rustling from within and Bess wondered what sort of tailor could possibly be small enough to fit inside a hatbox. The next moment, the lid flipped open and a bright green head poked up over the top.

Bess stared in amazement. Penelope's head really was *bright* green – the most luminous shade one could imagine. It looked like she would glow in the dark. Bess didn't need to ask what kind of creature Penelope was. She was quite clearly an alien. Back at the Odditorium there was a display about local UFO sightings and Pops had put a plastic model of an alien next to it.

When Penelope scrambled up to sit on the edge of the hatbox, Bess saw that she looked exactly like that alien model although she was smaller – about the size of a large cat. She was green from head to toe and just like the model she had a large head, two enormous eyes that took up most of her face and extremely long fingers. But, unlike the model, Penelope was wearing clothes: a lacy pink nightie with lots of ruffles and a magnificent pair of slippers shaped like bunny rabbits with floppy ears.

"Penny, this is Bess," Beau said. "She's joining the train for a while."

"Hello." Bess stepped forward, fascinated and desperate to know more about Penelope. "Your clothes are beautiful."

The alien gazed at her for a moment before reaching into her nightie pocket and pulling out a placard. She held it up so that Bess could read the single word printed on it: YES.

Bess beamed at Penelope. "How did you come to be here? What's your home planet like? Are things very different here on this world?"

Penelope jabbed her YES sign into the air again.

"I'm afraid you won't get much conversation from Penny," Beau said. "She understands our language perfectly, but she can't speak it. Her tongue is completely the wrong shape."

Penelope promptly opened her mouth and stuck out her tongue to demonstrate. It was very long and thin and forked at the end like a lizard's.

"I keep suggesting she make some more signs," Beau went on. "We could get a bit of variety into our conversation then. But Penny's more interested in making clothes than chatting. All we really know is that she crash-landed her flying saucer in our world about ten years ago and she liked it here so much that she decided to stay. She's been making clothes ever since.

And she is *very* good at it. The professor was delighted when she agreed to join the train."

"Well, I'm so happy to meet you, Penelope," Bess said.

The alien lifted her hand in acknowledgement.

"Have you had breakfast yet?" Beau asked.

Penelope flipped the sign round. On the other side was printed the word NO.

"They probably took your tray away," Beau said. "If you get a move on to the kitchen, you might still be able to get a croissant."

The alien promptly scrambled down the tower of hatboxes and shuffled off in her slippers, presumably in search of croissants.

"Penny is great as long as you're respectful and polite," Beau said as soon as the door closed behind her. "But if she ever catches you making fun of her then watch out for any clothing she gives you. Rumour has it she once made a pair of shoes that could freeze your feet solid, as well as a jacket that poured slime from its sleeves and a pair of gloves that made you slap yourself every time you were mean to someone."

"Oh, I wouldn't dream of making fun of her!" Bess exclaimed. "I think she's wonderful."

Beau grinned. "You know, I think you're going to fit right in here."

Bess felt a faint blush warm her skin and tried not to give away how pleased his words made her. She'd never really fitted in anywhere before and the thought of doing so here, in such a marvellous place, was beyond her wildest dreams. She silently thanked Pops for guiding her to the train and then headed after Beau as he continued his tour.

CHAPTER 18

Beau explained that the amber carriages were home to the teacup goblins, who could apparently be a bit jabby, and the eyeball plants, who were very possessive of their nests. There was also a second red carriage with a pretty little garden on its roof.

"What's in there?" Bess asked curiously.

Beau paused. "It's empty at the moment."

"Then why's it red?"

"Because it's...not always empty. Professor Ash thought it best that it just stays out of bounds all the time, to avoid confusion."

Before Bess could ask any more questions, Beau beckoned her through to another carriage and began introducing her to some of the people there. Bess tried to make a mental note of all their names, but her head was in a whirl and she wasn't sure she'd ever remember them all. Finally, Beau looped back to the sleeper carriages to show Bess where she was going to stay.

"There's only one bed free at the moment so I guess they've put you in Room Twelve with Maria." He stopped outside a compartment and rapped on the door. "Maria?" he called. "Can we come in?"

"Sure thing. Just watch out for the butterflies."

Beau pushed open the door and Bess gasped. The compartment was on fire! At least that's what it looked like to begin with, but then she saw it wasn't *on* fire as such, it was just full of flames – flames in the shape of giant butterflies that fluttered their blazing wings, shining red, orange and yellow.

In the middle of the butterflies stood a girl. Bess recognised her from the show. She was no longer wearing a sequinned costume, but a pair of red jeans and a white T-shirt with a picture of a little dragon stamped above the pocket. Her mass of curly black and red hair was tied up in a high ponytail. Her hands were stretched out in front of her and appeared to be controlling the butterflies.

Bess could feel the heat radiating from them, yet Maria didn't look at all hot herself, despite the fact that she was surrounded by fire. When Bess had seen her at the show, she'd assumed Maria was some kind of fire performer, but she realised the girl was much more than that – she was magical. Now that her arms were bare, Bess saw that Maria had intricate swirling patterns on her skin that looked like tiny leaves and flowers. They glowed bright red, but faded away into nothing when Maria suddenly clapped her hands. The fire butterflies disappeared in a puff of smoke.

Maria looked at Bess and grinned. "Hello! I've heard a lot about you this morning. You must be quite a talented thief if you managed to break into the train *and* get past Beau's ninja mice. You didn't seem like a thief when you were telling off that horrible boy last night. Nice necklace, by the way."

"Thanks," Bess replied. Her hand automatically went to the little bottle of ghost pepper. No one had ever complimented it before. "I'm not a thief though. I was never going to steal anything. I just really needed to speak to Professor Ash. Oh, and I like your dragon T-shirt."

Beau laughed. "It's not a picture," he said. "He's a real dragon."

Bess did a double take. What she had thought was a printed dragon's head poking out of the pocket actually was a real red dragon. As she stared, he crawled out of the pocket and settled himself on Maria's shoulder, sighing out a little puff of smoke in contentment. About the size of a mouse, he was small but perfect in every way, from the tips of his spiny wings to the end of his lizardy snout.

"Oh, he's…he's fantastic!" Bess exclaimed.

"Would you like to hold him?" Maria offered.

"I'd *love* to!"

Maria scooped the dragon off her shoulder and set him down in Bess's outstretched hands. He pattered to and fro, sniffing and snuffling at her thumb for a moment before flicking out his little tongue to give her a quick lick.

"That means he likes you!" Maria said. "And if Cedric likes you then I do too."

"Cedric? Is that his name?"

Bess grinned down at the dragon. She'd always wanted a pet and was forever asking her parents, but the answer had consistently been no. Bess was glad to have Blizzard in her life at least, but it wasn't quite the same. After all, she couldn't actually touch the alligator without him trying to bite her fingers off.

It was suddenly hard to believe that less than twenty-four hours ago she had been sitting at home, bored out of her mind by a jigsaw puzzle and longing for adventures. She'd barely been with the train more than five minutes and already she'd eaten a hot frog, ridden an enchanted carousel horse and held a dragon.

"I'm a fire witch," Maria explained. "Cedric is my familiar."

Their conversation was interrupted just then by the train giving three sharp blasts on its whistle.

Toot, toot, toot!

Beau and Maria exchanged an excited look and the dragon leaped from Bess's hand to fly back to Maria's shoulder.

"The whistles mean we're at the gateway!" Beau said to Bess. "The door to the Land of Halloween Sweets! Quick, if we hurry to the roof, then we might see it."

ChapTER 19

The train had rolled to a stop, which made it easier for Bess to keep her balance as she hurried down the corridor after Beau and Maria. They went to the end of the carriage and climbed the ladder attached to the outside. It seemed that everyone else on board the train was eager to see the door too because it was quite crowded up on the roof. Indeed, there were people standing on every roof, all straining to glimpse what lay ahead.

They were still within a tunnel, but now mossy chandeliers hung from the ceiling of earth above them. Bess could see thick roots winding down the sides as if some gigantic trees were stationed directly above. When she said as much to Beau, he nodded and replied, "Those are redwoods."

"Redwoods?"

"The giant trees in Sequoia."

Bess had seen photos of them back at the Odditorium. They were the largest trees in the world and incredibly old – they'd even existed during dinosaur times.

"But Sequoia National Park is all the way in California," she said.

"That's right." Beau grinned. "Professor Ash might have mentioned the short cuts? It doesn't take that long to get to California when you're travelling by troll tunnel. Anyway, one of the gateways to the other worlds is directly underneath the redwood trees in the national park. There are several gateways that we know about – they all have timetables at Dark Central Station, telling you which world is coming up next."

"And what about all these?" Bess pointed to the signs lining the walls of the tunnel. There were various warnings written on them in a spiky scrawl: *Danger!* and *Turn back!* and *Beware!*

"Up ahead is a gateway to other worlds," Maria said with a grin. "Only the boldest adventurers would willingly go through it. You never know quite what you're going to find on the other side."

"Sometimes it's a monster with hundreds of eyes that wants to gobble you up," Beau put in cheerfully.

"Really?" Bess was startled.

"That only happened once," said a mild voice behind them.

Bess turned to see that Louie had joined them on the carriage roof. He'd changed out of his dressing gown and now wore a pair of dark trousers and a smart grey waistcoat. He still had on his green train slippers though.

"Come on," Beau said. "Let's get closer to the front. I want to see the gate."

The four children weaved their way past the adults until they were at the rails right at the front of the first carriage, with the train engine directly before them. From here, they could see a tunnel up ahead. It wasn't illuminated so the entrance just looked like a big black hole. There was a signal crossing at the entrance with a long wooden bar blocking the way forward.

"I thought there was going to be a door," Bess said, frowning.

"It hasn't got here yet," Louie said, taking a handsome gold pocket watch from his waistcoat and flipping open the case. Bess saw that the watch inside was an unusual one, displaying the phases of the moon. "It's due to arrive in one minute, according to the almanac."

"There was a different door there before," Maria explained. "What was it again, Beau? The Land of Chatty Acorns or something like that?"

"The Land of Talking Trees," Beau replied.

"Right. The Land of Talking Trees. Well, that was there for a couple of weeks, I think, but then it moved on. Now we're in that gap between the old world leaving and the new one arriving. That's why the signal-crossing gate is down."

"What would happen if the train went through the tunnel before the door arrived?" Bess asked.

Maria glanced towards the dark entrance. "You'd get lost between the worlds."

"That doesn't sound good," Bess said.

"There's only a few known cases of anyone going into the tunnel when it was between doors," Louie said. "But, in every case, the person was never heard from again. Oh, look! The gate's arriving!"

A light on the signal crossing had started to flash and the next moment a spectacular sparkling gate slid into view with a *clang* that echoed down the tunnel. It was as if it had suddenly rolled out from the tunnel wall. A hush fell as everyone craned forward to get a better look.

The gate reminded Bess of the ones at the entrance to Roseville's cemetery. Large and grand, they were painted a shiny black and had pointed tips at the top. But, unlike the cemetery gates, this one was adorned with a selection of spooky little dolls.

There was a witch and a vampire, a bandaged mummy and a red demon, a black cat and a bat, and many others. There was a lot of purple and black in the clothing and the dolls' eyes were all made of different-sized buttons. Not only that, but they each had a lumpy, misshapen sort of look to them, which reminded Bess of photos she'd seen of cursed poppets. She loved them at once and wished she could have a set of them lined up on a shelf in her bedroom. They were much more appealing than the blue-eyed dolls with blonde ringlets that she'd seen sitting gormlessly in the window of Roseville's toyshop.

The light on the signal crossing stopped flashing and a bell rang out. Then the barrier lifted up and there was nothing between the train and the gate. Everyone watched as Professor Ash stepped down from the train and walked across the tracks. He put his hand on the gate and gave it a gentle push. It swung backwards with a soft squeaking of rusty hinges. Everyone on the roof breathed a sigh of relief.

"Sometimes the gates are padlocked when they arrive," Beau said to Bess. "Or else there's some charm or enchantment on them that means you can't get through. You never know for sure whether you'll be able to open them or not."

Bess watched as Professor Ash returned to the train. A moment later, the whistle tooted, steam chugged from the funnel and the train was grinding into life and moving towards the gate.

ChAPTER 20

Bess had assumed the tunnel would be much like the ones they'd travelled through before, so she was surprised when they passed through the gate to find it flanked by two gargoyles perched on pillars. They each held a platter of bat-shaped biscuits in their hands, which they offered up to the people on the train roof with a grunting noise. Bess wondered if the biscuits might make suitable food for her whispering flowers, but they didn't appear magical in any way. Everyone else was reaching over to help themselves, so Bess did the same, eager to try one.

"It can't be that dangerous a place," she said to the others. "Not if there's someone welcoming you with cookies at the entrance."

"Don't be so sure," Beau said, biting into his bat biscuit. "There was a penguin handing out ice lollies at the gate to Eyeball Monster Land."

"And a friendly little girl giving out gingerbread kittens at the Land of Sinking Swamps," Maria said. "We almost lost Mish there, didn't we? He flew straight into a swamp and was almost sucked to the bottom. Luckily Louie leaped in to save him. It was the bravest, stupidest thing I've ever seen."

"I couldn't let Mish drown in a swamp," Louie said. "I know he's always getting into mischief, but he's a sweet little soul."

"How long have you all been travelling on the train?" Bess asked. "It sounds like you've been on a lot of adventures together."

"Louie grew up here," Maria said. "Obviously, as it's his dad's train. I joined as a fire performer with my parents a few months ago. And Beau has been here for about a year. Ever since he ran away from ninja school."

"I did not run away from ninja school," Beau said calmly. "I've never set foot in a ninja school. I ran away from a theatre. I was an apprentice puppeteer."

Maria rolled her eyes. "Beau, it's the worst-kept secret on the train that you ran away from ninja school."

Beau shrugged. "I'm not sure where you're getting your information from, but it's completely false. You'd make a terrible spy."

"I think I'd make quite a *good* spy actually," Maria replied. "What with being a fire witch and all."

"Fire witches are too fond of fireworks and grand displays," Beau said. "Spies need to be still and silent – two things you couldn't be if you tried."

Louie offered Bess an apologetic smile. "I wish I could say they don't always bicker as much as this, but it wouldn't be true. I think they like each other underneath it all though."

"The point is that we've been on enough adventures to know looks can be deceptive when it comes to other worlds," Beau said. He turned to Bess and added, "So best keep your wits about you."

Bess intended to. They'd left the gargoyles behind now, which was a bit of a shame as those bat biscuits had been delicious, with tons of chocolate chips, and she would have quite liked a second. She made a mental note to offer something similar in the Odditorium's café, if she ever got the chance to open one.

Now the train was heading deeper into the tunnel, but it wasn't long and straight as Bess had expected. Instead, it curled down and around in a corkscrew shape like a helter-skelter. It was lit up with a warm orange glow from the hundreds of jack-o'-lanterns lining the walls. The pumpkins were all different shapes and sizes, nestled snugly together in little alcoves. As the train picked up speed, their grinning faces became something of a blur. It had been tricky enough to keep her balance before, but now Bess found it almost impossible.

"We should go back inside," Louie said.

They headed straight for the observation carriage. It was a very large space and, unlike the other carriages, it was made completely from glass. The walls, ceiling and even the floor were transparent, giving the occupants a clear view of whatever was outside. The seats all faced the windows.

Bess and the others sat down just as the train emerged from the corkscrew tunnel into a strange-looking land. It was a sunny day, but the sky wasn't blue like at home – it was bright purple with a few fluffy black clouds floating across the horizon.

A vista of fields stretched as far as Bess could see. At least she thought they were fields, but the blades of grass looked thick and jelly-like as if they were made from gummy worms. There were streams of bright blue jelly and the flowers were all black. A strong scent of liquorice filled the air and Bess thought maybe the flowers were edible. She spotted a couple of rabbits hopping about, but it was clear from their fangs and bloodshot eyes that they were werebunnies or vampire bunnies, or something along those lines.

Still, with the flowers, streams and rabbits, it might almost have been pretty if it weren't for the scarecrows. They were everywhere. Hundreds and hundreds of them. And they weren't small like the one Professor Ash had given Bess. These were even bigger than adults and rather threatening in their tattered rags. Bess hadn't seen any crows and wondered what they were supposed to be scaring away.

"If the ghostly gobstopper is where it's supposed to be, then it should be quite easy to find," Beau said.

He pulled a map from his pocket and Bess realised it was a hand-drawn copy of one of the ones she'd seen earlier in the almanac. He spread it out on his knees and the others leaned forward to take a look. The corkscrew entrance into the land was marked on the map, along with the area they were currently travelling through, which Bess saw was called the Scarecrow Fields.

"The gobstoppers are meant to be here, in the Forest of Chocolate Eyeballs." Beau pointed it out on the map. "And luckily for us, that's just on the other side of the Scarecrow Fields, where there's a train platform. We can reach it before dark and then hopefully locate the gobstopper and be on our way by the time the sun even sets."

"Hopefully," Louie said quietly. He glanced through the glass at the rows of scarecrows. "But things don't usually go to plan, do they? And the almanac's information is a hundred years old."

"Well, even if we have a few little detours, we still have three days and two nights here before the door back to our world disappears," Maria pointed out. "I'm sure we'll find the gobstopper in time."

The children lingered in the observation carriage, watching as the train chugged along in this strange land. Bess noticed that some of the scarecrows turned their large, misshapen heads to look at them as they passed by. But before long, the landscape up ahead changed – they had arrived at the Forest of Chocolate Eyeballs. A collection of gloomy-looking trees huddled together beneath the purple sky and from their twisted branches hung large eyeballs, blinking in the sunlight.

ChAPTER 21

The train came to a stop at a station just outside the forest. There was no sign of any other trains. In fact, there was no sign of any people at the station at all. It seemed quite deserted as if no one had been there for a very long time. The paint was peeling from the walls and the tracks were rusty.

"It's probably a haunted station," Beau said, looking at the map again. "Come on, let's check it out."

The children left the carriage and stepped on to the platform. Many of the adults from the train did the same, including Maria's parents. She introduced them to Bess and they greeted her warmly. Professor Ash joined them on the platform a moment later.

"Anyone who would like to explore the Forest of Chocolate Eyeballs is free to do so," he said to the group. "But please come back to the train at once when you hear the whistle give three toots to signal that it's ready to leave. Whoever finds a ghostly gobstopper first, if you would be so kind as to return to the train and ask the driver to sound the whistle twice. And of course, as always, if you hear the train whistle give one long blast, then that means there is serious peril and you must run back to the safety of the train as fast as you can. Other than that, I hope you all enjoy your visit here."

"Back in a jiffy," Beau said. "I just need to fetch my puppet coat." He slipped back into the train before Bess could ask what this was.

"I should get my bag too," Louie said, following him.

Maria turned to her parents. "Can I go and look for the gobstopper with them?"

"As long as you're careful," her mum replied. "And don't go anywhere by yourself. Make sure there's an adult in your group."

It looked to Bess as if about half the people from the train were staying on board and the other half were planning to explore.

"A lot of folk prefer to see new lands from the windows," Maria told Bess when she asked why her parents were staying behind. "And some, like my mum and dad, aren't really that fussed about exploring at all.

They joined the train because it was a good job for all of us, with food and board thrown in. They usually stay on the train whenever it stops, practising their act. Luckily they don't mind if I go off exploring. I'd be bored stiff sitting on there all day."

Beau came back just then, wearing a long black coat that reached almost to his ankles.

"Is that another one of Penelope's creations?" Bess asked.

"Nope. Just an ordinary coat," Beau replied. "Except for the fact that it has a lot of pockets." He opened it up to display three large pockets on either side, each with a puppet dangling from the top.

"Dad's ready," Louie said, appearing beside them. "He said we can go with him."

Bess saw that Louie had his violin case on a strap slung over his shoulder. Together they walked over to where Professor Ash was lacing up a pair of walking boots.

"Hello, all," he said. "Are we ready to venture into the forest? The almanac doesn't give too much detail so best keep a sharp eye out, just in case."

"In case of what?" Bess asked.

"Well, I don't wish to alarm you, but one never knows what one might find when exploring new worlds," the professor said. "Everything can appear quite safe and peaceful one moment, but then it can all get a bit frantic when an octopus drops out of the sky on to your head."

Bess glanced up at the sky, but there was no sign of any octopuses. For now at least.

Professor Ash led the way into the forest. The trees had a swampy look about them with branches that twisted and turned outwards to create a great canopy like a green ceiling. It blocked out a lot of the sunlight, but there were more jack-o'-lanterns nestled between the branches or piled up at the base of the tree trunks. The orange glow from their candles provided plenty of light.

The most peculiar thing about the place was the chocolate eyeballs. They hung down from every tree on long vines. They were quite large – about the size of Bess's hand – and they had chocolate eyelashes as well as eyelids that blinked slowly at them as they walked by. It was rather odd being stared at by a tree. Bess had no idea whether the forest was happy for them to be there or not.

The smell of chocolate was rich and intense in the air, as if they'd just walked into a chocolate factory. It made Bess's stomach rumble, especially when she noticed that some of the eyeballs were white chocolate, which was her favourite. Chocolate eyeballs certainly seemed like they'd fit the bill when it came to the whispering flowers too, but Bess shuddered at the thought of plucking one. They seemed alive after all and Bess was pretty sure that they wouldn't like being removed from their trees.

"Do we know exactly where in the forest the gobstoppers are meant to be?" she asked.

She spoke in a whisper, but all the nearby eyeballs still swivelled round on their vines to stare at her, which was a little unsettling.

"There's supposed to be a particularly tall tree somewhere," Professor Ash replied. "Apparently the ghostly gobstoppers are right at the top. That's where the candy crows have their nests, you see."

"Candy crows?"

"Black birds about this big." Professor Ash held up his hands to demonstrate a bird roughly the size of a normal crow back in their world. "They're perfectly harmless. But they're very partial to ghostly gobstoppers and they collect them to feed their young. There are meant to be dozens of gobstoppers up there so I'm sure they won't notice if we take just one."

"What else lives in the forest?" Maria asked.

"According to the almanac, the candy crows are the only creatures here."

"So the almanac didn't mention anything about dinosaurs?" Bess put in.

Professor Ash looked puzzled. "Not that I can recall. I'm fairly certain I would remember if there had been any suggestion of dinosaurs. Why do you ask?"

"Because something made that footprint."

Bess pointed. A little way ahead there was a gigantic dinosaur-shaped footprint stamped into the crumbly soil.

Chapter 22

Everyone gathered round the massive footprint and stared.

"A candy crow definitely didn't make that," Beau said. "It's bigger than me."

He demonstrated by lying down in the footprint, which was indeed longer and wider than him.

"It does look like a dinosaur footprint," Louie said, frowning at it.

Bess glanced around nervously. It was a bit worrying to think that a dinosaur might come stomping through the trees at any moment.

"Here, let me see what Jemima makes of it." Beau got to his feet and reached into his coat to pull out a puppet.

Like the others, this one was made entirely from felt, with long fluffy black hair tied back beneath a pith helmet. She wore a khaki shirt and belted trousers paired with chunky walking boots.

Beau began to move his hand, just as Bess had seen him do back at Roseville, as if he were manipulating a traditional puppet on strings. Jemima immediately sprang to life and Beau's hand dropped to his side as the puppet scrambled into the footprint and started examining it from every angle.

"Jemima is a zoologist," Beau said, glancing at Bess. "She's pretty good at identifying animals."

After a few moments, Jemima walked over to Beau. She reached into the pocket of her shirt and drew out a book. It was quite tiny and everyone leaned forward as she flicked quickly through the pages before holding the book up for them to see the picture of the animal printed there.

"An eagle?" Bess looked back down at the footprint. "But eagles don't get as big as that, do they?"

"Not in our world," Professor Ash replied. "But anything is possible here."

"Do you think that's what all those scarecrows were for?" Maria asked.

"Quite possibly," the professor said. "At any rate, this rather changes things. The only responsible course of action is for you children to return to the train right away. Why, an eagle this large could carry you clean aw—"

Before he could finish his sentence, they all heard the raucous cry of a bird directly overhead. When they looked up, the canopy of leaves was too thick to see anything, but Bess thought she saw the flickering shadow of something massive.

"Goodness me, what are you people doing here?" a little voice asked.

They looked round to see a fairy perched on the branch of a nearby tree. She wore a Halloween dress in purple and black, with a pointed witch's hat on her head and a tiny broomstick in her hand. She was staring at them with an expression of horror.

"You must leave at once!" she said. "This forest is only safe for witch fairies and pumpkins. Anything else is in danger from the Easter eagles."

Bess glanced at the others, but she could tell from their expressions that they were as confused as she was.

"Easter eagles?" Professor Ash repeated.

"Don't tell me you've never heard of them?" the witch fairy exclaimed. "Why, the Easter eagles are cousins of the Easter bunny!"

"The Easter bunny isn't so bad," Beau said, scooping up Jemima and stuffing her back into his coat pocket.

The fairy shook her head. "Why do you think they're not in the Land of Easter Eggs where they belong? The Easter bunny banished them. Threw them out for good."

"How come?" Beau asked with another glance up at the leaves.

"You don't want to find out. Just go back wherever it is you came from at once!"

"I'm afraid that's not an option," Professor Ash said. "We're here on a very important mission, you see. We need to find a ghostly gobstopper, which I believe is located in the nest of a candy crow?"

But the witch fairy was shaking her head. "There haven't been any ghostly gobstoppers here for years. The Easter eagles gobbled them up, along with all the candy crows."

Professor Ash's face fell. He glanced at Louie for a moment before turning back to the fairy. "But...are you saying that there are no ghostly gobstoppers left in this land at *all*?"

"Yes. Well, except for the one in the Candymaker's collection of course, but you won't get anywhere near that."

A loud screech cut through the air and they all jumped. The eagle was definitely getting closer.

"*Please* leave," the witch fairy begged. "Get yourselves to safety, if it's not already too late. The eyes will have told the eagles where you are by now. They'll be looking for you."

Before they could ask the fairy any more questions, she hopped on to her broomstick and flew away. Bess was suddenly very aware of the chocolate eyeballs surrounding them, all blinking that slow, silent stare. She didn't know how or why, but it appeared that the fairy was right – they were able to communicate with the Easter eagles. Suddenly it seemed like a sensible idea to get back to the train as quickly as possible.

"Come along," Professor Ash said, sounding nervous. "There's no point lingering here if there are no gobstoppers. How fast can you run?"

They raced back through the forest. Some of the other exploring groups must have been warned about the eagles too because, just then, the train gave one long blast on its whistle, signalling danger. Bess and the others were almost out of the trees now, but the eyeballs swivelled on their vines to look at them wherever they went.

The birds descended on them as soon as they left the treeline. The Train of Dark Wonders was *right there*, so close and yet impossibly far away. Two eagles were swooping down, both monstrously big with cold, pitiless yellow eyes and cruel, sharp beaks. Their feathers were a mix of pretty pastel colours, but they were dirty and ragged and jutted out at messy angles with old bits of chocolate wrappers and half-chewed sweets stuck in them. The birds looked as if they'd crawled out of a massive bin.

But they could move with lightning speed. Bess barely had time to realise what was happening before one of the eagles clamped its enormous claw round her middle and lifted her clean off the ground.

ChaPTeR 23

The forest fell away from Bess as she dangled helplessly in the eagle's claw. The bird had snatched Maria up with its other claw, while the second eagle had scooped up Beau and Louie. Professor Ash was shouting something down below, but the birds had such huge wings that after only a couple of flaps they were soaring high above the train and towards the horizon. They were moving so fast that Bess's eyes streamed.

"This isn't good!" Maria shouted over to her. "This is definitely *not* where we want to be."

Bess gripped on to the eagle's tough talon until her knuckles turned white. She was terrified that the bird might suddenly drop her, yet at the same time she couldn't help being just a *little* bit thrilled at the sight of the Land of Halloween Sweets spread out below.

Being snatched away by a giant eagle sounded like the type of adventure Pops might have told her about. The kind of story that she could never be completely sure was actually true or not.

"Can't you use your fire magic?" Bess called to Maria. She could see Cedric clinging on to the witch's shoulders.

"Not while we're flying," Maria replied. "The eagle might drop us if I try anything. We've got no choice but to let it land first."

Bess twisted her head to look back at the second eagle swooping along behind them, Beau and Louie gripped in its claws. The boys had obviously had the same thought as Maria because they weren't making any attempt to escape either. When Bess stared back down at the landscape below, she saw that they'd already flown far away from the Forest of Chocolate Eyeballs. In fact, it wasn't even in view any more.

It seemed like most of the land was made up of various graveyards with crooked, rundown churches, in among forests, fields and vegetable patches. There were some rocky-looking mountains up ahead and, in the distance, Bess saw the ruins of a pink castle. But there was no sign of any people. No shops or schools or houses…

At least there was *one* house, but it was really more of a mansion. A gigantic black marble building in the middle of a large gated garden, complete with its own fountains and even a maze. Bess marvelled at it as they flew over, wondering if this could be the home of the Candymaker the witch fairy had mentioned. There was a strange-looking orange forest just beyond the mansion's gates, but before Bess could take a proper look the eagles swooped down towards the mountains.

"Get ready!" Maria called. "I think we're finally going to land—" But then she broke off with a shocked cry.

Bess peered down and saw that they were headed straight for a massive eagle's nest tucked into a ledge high up on the side of one of the mountains. There were bits of sweet wrappers and pieces of golden chocolate foil stuck between the twigs. And the nest was full of Easter eaglets. They all seemed extremely hungry because they were throwing their little bald heads back and opening their beaks as wide as they would go.

Bess felt a rush of dismay. The next second, the eagle threw the girls into the nest. Luckily it was fairly soft although it smelled dreadful – like dirty feathers and rotten breath. Bess and Maria tumbled in without hurting themselves and the two boys crashed down next to them a moment later.

As the children scrambled to their feet, they saw that there were five eaglets altogether and they were as tall as they were. The baby eagles were mostly bald with only a feather or two attached to their wrinkly pink skin. They had the same staring yellow eyes as their parents and their beaks looked terribly sharp. They crowded round the children in excitement, letting out piercing squawks. The adult eagles circled away, probably to go and find more food.

"Did you bring your sword-fighting puppet?" Louie gasped, nudging Beau in the ribs.

"No! I didn't think we'd need to do any sword-fighting in a land of sweets!"

"Leave it to me, boys," Maria said, already rolling up her sleeves. "I'll get us out of this mess as usual."

The boldest eaglet lunged at Maria with a screech, but she threw up her hands and yelled, "Stay back!"

An arc of fire shot from her palms and formed into a ball. The next instant, the ball morphed into the shape of a ferocious-looking lion, which bellowed out a great, fearsome roar. Bess could feel the intense heat blasting off it and the eaglets obviously could too because they all stumbled back to the edge of the nest, squawking in dread.

For a moment, Bess was afraid that the lion might set the entire nest on fire and she really didn't want that to happen. The eaglets were fierce and clearly very much wanted to eat them, but they were still only babies and just following their nature. The last thing Bess wanted was to see them all burned to a crisp. But fortunately the lion's fire magic seemed to be contained within itself – just like the butterflies back at the train – and it didn't so much as shed a spark.

"Come on," Maria said. "Let's make our escape before the parents come back."

The children hauled themselves out of the nest, leaving the fire lion standing guard.

Chapter 24

"**H**ow long have we got until the fire lion disappears?" Bess asked as they slipped and scrambled their way down a steep mountain path as fast as they could. They were extremely high above the ground and Bess was glad she wasn't afraid of heights.

"Probably five minutes or so," Maria replied. "He'll fizzle out if I get too far away, but hopefully it won't matter by then."

They carried on for what felt like forever until they were all very hot and out of breath.

"Right," Beau finally said. "We must have gone far enough by now to take a break. It feels like we've been running away from things all day."

The children collapsed on the stony path in an exhausted heap.

"That lion was amazing," Bess said to Maria. She hesitated and then her next words came out in a rush. "I think you're the coolest person I've ever met."

Maria looked taken aback by the praise, but then she gave a brilliant smile. "Well, thanks. You should see my fire shark. He's pretty special too."

"The lion wasn't bad," Beau admitted. "But I still don't think it can compare to my gunslinger puppet."

"Well, your gunslinger puppet isn't here, is she?" Maria replied. "And she didn't just save us all from a bunch of Easter eaglets."

"That was great work, Maria," Louie said. "Well done. We're not out of danger yet though. It's really very serious that we've been separated from the others like this. We don't even have much in the way of supplies. I've only got my violin."

"I brought six puppets," Beau said. "The zoologist, the magician, the archer, the princess and one of the ninja mice." He looked over at Louie. "And the wolf whisperer of course."

"I didn't bring anything except Cedric," Maria put in.

"I've got a lock-picking kit," Bess said, patting her pocket to make sure it was still there. She wished she had something more spectacular to offer. "Well, and the ghost pepper in my necklace. And the pressed tree in my backpack, but that's only useful if it starts growing apples again. Should we try to make our way back to the Forest of Chocolate Eyeballs?"

Louie shook his head. "The witch fairy said the only place we'd find a ghostly gobstopper is in the Candymaker's collection, so that's where my dad will go. We should try to meet back up with him there."

"I saw a black marble mansion as we were flying here," Bess said. "Do you think that could be the Candymaker's house?"

"Perhaps." Louie turned to Beau. "Do you remember what the almanac said about him?"

"Only that he's meant to be the most dangerous thing in this land," Beau said grimly. "There's a legend that this world started out as something else, but then the Candymaker moved in and made all these Halloween sweets and they took over."

"Well, it sounds like we should probably stay away from his house then," Bess said. "There's loads of other cool stuff here that would make a great addition to the train. It doesn't have to be the ghostly gobstopper, does it?"

She expected the others to agree with her. After all, there was going on a fun adventure and then there was just being silly by walking into certain danger. But, to her surprise, the trio exchanged glances and went quiet.

"What is it?" Bess asked. "There's something you're not telling me. Why is the ghostly gobstopper so important?"

Beau looked at Louie. "It's up to you, but we probably *should* tell her. I mean, she's going to find out at some point. I know you're always nervous to open up about this, but…well, we can all see that Bess is a bit strange like us. No offence, by the way," he added, smiling at her. "I think being strange is a good thing." He turned back to Louie. "I'm sure we can help her understand."

"Understand what?" Bess said. She was burning with curiosity by now.

Louie sighed and gave her an apologetic look. "There's, um, something you ought to know about me. But, before I tell you, I'd just like you to know that I honestly don't want to hurt anyone or anything. I mean, even flies and mosquitoes and so on have a right to live and are just trying to go about their business. I'd never dream of squashing one. So I really hope that you won't be afraid of me when I tell you that I'm… Well, the fact is that I'm a little bit cursed. Perhaps if I explain it all from the beginning I might—"

"Er, Louie?" Maria suddenly said sharply. "I don't think we have time for that. Have you looked at your watch since we arrived?"

"Well, no, but the sun's still high in the sky so…"

Louie trailed off as they all looked up. The sun *had* been high in the sky just a short while ago, but now it was sinking fast – much faster than at home. Bess guessed that the sun's cycle must be different here. They were in another world after all. Anything might be possible.

The sunset had an alarming effect on Louie. The small amount of colour in his face drained away and he fumbled for his pocket watch. His hands trembled as he flipped open the lid and stared at the clock with a horrified expression.

"Why are you looking at that?" Bess asked, puzzled. "Does time even work in the same way here?"

She didn't know what was going on, but she had the feeling that something terrible was about to happen.

"The watch is enchanted," Louie said hoarsely. "It measures the time and moon cycles of whichever world it's in." He looked up and stared at Beau. "A full moon is going to rise in the next few minutes. We're too late."

He'd barely finished speaking before the sun sank below the horizon altogether. The sky turned pink and red and then a flurry of bats burst from one of the mountain caves overhead. Moments later, a pale sliver of moon peeped over the horizon, getting larger and larger by the second. It looked as if that was going to rise much faster than it did at home too.

"Is anyone going to tell me what's going—" Bess began.

But that was as far as she got before Maria took her hand and squeezed it hard. "Stay close to me," she said in a low voice. "And don't scream. That will only make him angry."

"What? Why would I scream?" Bess asked. "And who would be angry?"

But Maria didn't have time to reply because events happened very quickly then. The sky lost its remaining red, which was replaced with inky blackness, spreading as fast as paint mixing with water. Louie hastily shrugged his violin case from his shoulder and shoved it across the ground to Maria, who picked it up and swung it on to her back. Beau reached into his coat as the full moon climbed higher in the sky. He grabbed a puppet and threw it on the ground just as the moon came to a stop, flooding the land below with silvery light.

Louie doubled over as if he had tummy ache. Bess looked on in astonishment as his nails lengthened into claws and ice-white fur spread out across his skin. His body changed shape before her eyes and his nose lengthened into a long snout. Suddenly there was no longer a boy standing before them at all but a white wolf.

"Don't panic," Maria said calmly. "And whatever you do, don't run. The fact is that Louie is a werewolf."

CHAPTER 25

Bess remained frozen to the spot. Louie's eyes were still grey, but where there had been gentleness in them before, there was now only wildness. His clothes had all been shredded and were lying in a heap at his feet. He was snarling, teeth bared, a thin line of drool dangling from the edge of his lip, and there was a coiled energy in his body as if he were about to pounce. He looked so frightening that Bess could feel a scream tickling the back of her throat and she had to clench her teeth to stop it from coming out.

Beau raised his hands and began to manipulate the puppet he'd thrown to the ground. It was a man in a long white trench coat that reached to his ankles. His fluffy blond puppet hair was swept back from his head to reveal a wolf-fang earring dangling from his right ear. The puppet moved slowly forward, hands outstretched in a calming gesture.

To Bess's surprise and relief, this seemed to have an instant effect on Louie, who stopped snarling and lay down instead. The wolf's eyes remained fixed on them, but at least he didn't look like he was about to attack at any moment. He even let the puppet pick up his tattered clothing and toss it back to Beau, who stuffed it into one of his coat pockets.

"The puppet is a wolf whisperer," Maria said quietly to Bess. "Back on the train we have a special carriage with a cage in it and Louie goes in that whenever it's a full moon."

"The other red carriage?" Bess whispered back.

"Yes," Maria replied, keeping her eyes fixed on Louie. "We all hate seeing him in a cage, but it's the only way to be completely safe. The wolf-whisperer puppet helps a bit, but it's not completely reliable. There was another puppet before this one, you see, and Louie… Well, he ate it."

"Come on," Beau said. "Let's find shelter while the puppet's magic is working."

Bess followed the other two further down the steep mountain path, picking their way slowly in the moonlight. Louie crept after the puppet in a slinking prowl behind them.

"Remember, whatever you do, don't run," Beau said softly. "Louie will definitely attack if you do. It's not his fault. He can't help himself when he's a wolf."

"That's why we need the ghostly gobstopper," Maria explained. "It will let Louie remain himself when he turns into a wolf. He'll be in control and won't hurt anyone so he won't have to go in the cage any more."

Before too long, the children found a small mountain cave and the three of them piled in, leaving the puppet outside with Louie. As an extra precaution, Maria summoned a gate made of fire to bar the entrance.

"Just in case Louie eats the whisperer puppet again," she said.

They watched Louie prowling up and down, with the puppet standing guard by the gate. After a little while, Louie seemed to get bored. He turned and ran off down the mountain, giving an eerie wolf howl that made the hairs on Bess's arms stand on end.

"He'll probably be gone all night," Beau said. "Hunting rabbits or whatever they have in the Land of Halloween Sweets."

"I saw some rabbits earlier," Bess said. "In the Scarecrow Fields. They had little fangs so I think they might have been wererabbits."

"They ought to keep Louie busy then," Maria said. "We'll find him again in the morning."

"What happened to him?" Bess asked. "How did he become cursed?"

"He was bitten by a werewolf when he was little," Maria replied. "In one of the other worlds. Professor Ash has tried everything to cure him, but so far we haven't found anything that can undo the curse."

"But the ghostly gobstopper can help him stay in control when he's a wolf?" Bess said.

"That's right." Beau nodded. "That's why it's so important that we find it, even if it means going into the Candymaker's mansion itself." He looked at Bess. "You can stay outside when we get there. Louie is our friend, but you barely know him. It wouldn't be fair to ask you to put yourself in danger."

Bess tried not to wince. She liked Beau, Maria and Louie very much and it hurt a little bit to be reminded that she wasn't part of their group, that she was only a guest who had come along for the ride. The other three children were all extraordinary and interesting in some way – like the fascinating people Bess might read about in the pages of one of Pops's books. At school, Bess had always felt a little bit odd, but here she had never felt more plain and ordinary.

"I know Louie isn't my friend," she said tentatively, "but I'd still like to help him if I can. I don't have any of your spectacular talents, but I'm really very good at lock-picking. And the Candymaker's mansion will probably have plenty of locked doors, won't it? I can help with that at least."

Bess wanted to suggest that if they all worked together in the Land of Halloween Sweets then perhaps they might become real friends by the end of it all. She could think of nothing she'd like more. But suddenly she felt too shy, and worried that she might look a bit desperate, especially since Maria already knew that she had an unhappy time at school.

"Besides, I'd really like to see the mansion," Bess said instead. "It sounds fascinating. And I still need to find a way to save the Odditorium. Maybe there'll be something in the Candymaker's collection I can feed to the flowers."

"Okay." Beau shrugged. "If you're sure. You're probably right about the locks and we'll need all the help we can get."

"How come you have your own museum anyway?" Maria asked. "Aren't you a bit young?"

Bess explained how her grandfather had left it to her in his will, how she'd always loved the place and had big plans of her own for it. She then described some of the exhibits, her voice full of pride, especially when she got to Blizzard.

"An albino alligator?" Maria said, raising both eyebrows. "Wow, I'd certainly love to see that. Perhaps we can come and visit when we get back?"

"You're all welcome any time," Bess said. "Free of charge. It would be wonderful to have visitors who appreciate the curiosities for a change."

Beau's stomach gave a rumble just then and he sighed. "I don't know about you two, but I'm starving."

They briefly considered venturing from the cave to search for food, but then decided it was best not to in case Louie was still prowling about out there.

"It'll be safe by morning," Beau said. "And we can have sweets for breakfast."

CHAPTER 26

Bess had never slept in a cave before and she found the hard, stony floor quite uncomfortable, especially as the only pillow she had was her backpack. But there was no way she would have traded it for being safely back home in her bed. She loved the strangeness of her situation, especially when she saw a flurry of bats pass by the mouth of the cave and heard an eerie wolf's howl, which she guessed came from Louie.

Once the sun had risen, Maria took down the fire gate and Beau tucked the wolf-whisperer puppet back in his coat. Then he put Louie's clothes outside in a pile.

"But aren't those shredded to bits?" Bess asked him, remembering how Louie's wolf body had torn through them.

"Yes, but all of Louie's clothes are made by Penelope and she werewolf-proofs them," Beau said. "As soon as he picks them up, they stitch themselves back together again."

Sure enough, a short while later, Louie appeared in the cave wearing his old outfit, which seemed quite unchanged. The same couldn't be said for Louie, whose blond hair stuck up at funny angles like Beau's. His skin was streaked with dust and dirt, and he looked seriously in need of a good bath.

"Sorry I didn't tell you earlier," he said to Bess. "I just didn't want you to be scared of me."

"That's okay," Bess replied. "It's your secret so it's up to you who you share it with. I'm not scared of you though."

Louie's face lit up. "You're not?"

"No. I mean, I'm a little bit afraid of your wolf, but I'm not afraid of *you*."

"I'm glad," Louie said. "When I'm a wolf, I can't tell who my friends are. You all just look like…food. Really tasty food too, I mean. Not broccoli or anything like that, but loaded fries or a double cheeseburger or—"

"I get the idea," Bess said hurriedly.

"But if we can get hold of a ghostly gobstopper then you won't need to be afraid of the wolf either."

"Speaking of which, we should get going," Beau said. "It's probably going to take us most of the morning to get to the bottom of this mountain."

They paused long enough to have breakfast at a nearby bush growing candy beetles. Bess had never had sweets for breakfast before and enjoyed it very much, even if the meal was a bit rushed. Then the four children hurried on down the path. It was rough and uneven and it certainly seemed as if not many people went this way.

They passed several more caves full of bats, with a strong smell of liquorice wafting from each one. They soon realised why when a stray bat fluttered into their path. Unlike Mish, these animals weren't made from fur and bone, but from sugar and liquorice. And instead of the usual bat droppings inside the cave, the floor was covered with liquorice allsorts.

"If the liquorice bats poop out liquorice allsorts, I wonder what the wererabbits' poo is like?" Bess wondered out loud.

"Perhaps we'll find out," Beau said grimly. "There's quite a bit of ground to cover before we reach the Candymaker's mansion."

As they got to the bottom half of the mountain, the bat caves gave way to spider caves. The children couldn't see any spiders, but they knew they must live there because of the massive webs filling up most of the space inside. Bess didn't like to think about how big the creatures who made them must be.

"The almanac mentioned that there were sugar spiders living in the mountains," Beau said, peering into the mouth of one of the caves as they walked past. "There isn't much more detail than that, but it's the reason I brought the princess puppet along."

"Why would a princess puppet be helpful?" Bess asked. She would have thought that an exterminator or bug-catcher puppet might have been a better choice.

"She's no ordinary princess," Beau said with a smile. "You'll see when you meet her. But she should come in handy if we find ourselves up against any spiders."

Even so, Bess was keen to avoid going inside a spider cave if they could help it. But, before long, the path they were following disappeared into one and there seemed to be no other way of moving forward.

Beau peered over the side of the mountain. "It's still too steep for us to climb or slide down."

"I guess that means we're just going to have to go through the cave," Maria said.

"We don't know that it will take us to the bottom of the mountain," Bess pointed out.

"It does," Louie said. "I went through it last night."

Bess was surprised. "You mean you remember everything you did?" Somehow she'd just assumed that Louie would have forgotten.

"Oh yes," he said quietly. "I remember everything. This cave leads to the field below the mountain. There's a spider in here somewhere. I didn't see it, but I could smell it. It must be huge because the webs are the biggest I've seen."

"Well, maybe the spider is asleep," Maria said. "And if not we can use Beau's puppet."

"The webs are made of sugar," Louie told them as they walked inside. "And the skeletons are made of fudge."

"Skeletons?" Bess repeated.

Louie pointed further into the cave, but everything was cloaked in shadow up ahead.

"We don't have your wolf eyesight," Maria said. "But perhaps my fire lion can help."

She muttered some magic words beneath her breath and a burst of fire shot from her hands. Once again, it morphed into the flaming, flickering shape of a lion. The huge fire beast padded ahead of them, leading the way deeper into the cave. By the light of its flames, Bess saw what Louie had been talking about.

There were skeletons dangling from the spider webs – their bones brown rather than white – and the sugary scent of fudge was strong in the air.

"They look human," Beau said, staring. "But what kind of people have fudge skeletons?"

"Hopefully we won't have to find out," Maria replied.

"Whatever they are, it's very tasty fudge," Louie said. "Sort of caramel-flavoured with a bit of a smoky, salty taste at the end." The others all looked at him and he blushed. "My wolf was hungry. At least I just ate bones rather than animals."

"Louie is a vegetarian most of the time," Maria put in.

As they walked on, the sugar webs sparkled in the light from the lion's flames. Bess couldn't help thinking that they looked very beautiful, even with the fudge skeletons grinning down at them in that unsettling way.

"Just a little bit further to go," Louie said after a while.

Bess knew he was right because she could see daylight filtering in from somewhere up ahead.

They were very nearly out of the cave when the spider appeared.

Chapter 27

They saw the spider's shadow first, moving across the cave wall up ahead in a skittering, scuttling motion. The children all stopped.

"Time for my princess puppet to do her thing," Beau said.

He reached into his coat and drew out the puppet. In the light from the lion's flames, Bess saw that she was unlike any princess she'd ever seen. There was no bright pink dress or tumbling locks of blonde hair. Instead, this princess wore a grey cobwebbed gown and delicate black lace gloves. A gleaming crown was perched upon her hair, which was long and silver, tied back with jewelled spider combs. Attached to the crown was a long black lace veil covered with intricate cobweb patterns, which ran all the way to the hem of her dress. The puppet had sparkling blue eyes and she wore a glittering spider ring upon one of her fingers.

Bess thought there was something serene and lovely about her, even though she was wearing cobwebs like they were silks. The puppet pattered forward on dainty slippered feet just as the spider dropped down before them on a long string of cobweb.

Bess had assumed Louie was right and that the spider must be huge, given the size of its webs. In fact, the creature was so small that Bess almost missed it – it was like a little diamond. But there wasn't just one spider – there were dozens and dozens of them. One by one, they descended silently from the roof of the cave on their webs, suspended in the air like sparkling raindrops. Bess felt the sudden urge to run her hands through her hair in case any had landed there, but they all seemed to have avoided the children.

They had surrounded them though and, as soon as Beau took a tentative step towards the exit, several of the spiders spun a web across his path with lightning speed. More spiders were doing the same behind them. Bess's heart sank as she realised there was no way of moving towards the exit or returning deeper into the cave without getting tangled up in the webs. She remembered the fudge skeletons and her heart beat faster at the thought that the sugar spiders might trap them too.

"A spiderweb will be no match for a fire lion," Maria said. "He can claw the way out for us."

The lion had raised its lips in a snarl and looked very much as if it wanted to do some clawing. But Louie laid a hand on Maria's shoulder. "Let Beau try with the puppet first. We're guests here. This is the spiders' home after all."

Maria rolled her eyes. "You were the one gobbling up their fudge skeletons last night, but okay – let's try it Beau's way. Hopefully we won't all get cobwebbed in the process."

The spiders *were* getting closer and closer to the children, and Bess's skin prickled with unease. She was quite certain that the spiders were about to start cocooning her at any moment and was starting to wish that they'd gone with Maria's plan.

But Beau seemed perfectly calm as he raised both hands in front of him to manipulate the princess puppet. "Watch and learn," he said. "Fire lions are all very well, but sometimes a bit of finesse is called for."

The puppet raised her gloved hands and began waving them gently through the air in front of her as if she were conducting an invisible orchestra.

The movement seemed to draw the spiders' attention to her for the first time and they all froze. The next instant, there was a flurry of activity. For a horrible, lurching moment, Bess thought it had all gone wrong and that the spiders were about to advance with renewed vigour.

Then she realised that they were actually dismantling the webs and were busily spinning something else instead. Within minutes, the cave was full of cobweb roses. They fell at the puppet princess's feet in a sparkling pile. She picked up one of the flowers, smiled serenely at the spiders and began gliding towards the exit.

"Well now," Beau said quietly with a smug glance at Maria, "isn't this better than burning everything to the ground? We should take the roses with us. They're meant as gifts and we wouldn't want to offend the spiders."

The children quickly gathered up the roses, which were white and sparkling and sticky in Bess's hands. Then they hurried after the puppet princess. The spiders made no move to stop them and soon enough they had emerged from the cave and were blinking in the sunlight.

"Looks like a puppet princess is just as useful as a fire lion after all," Beau remarked.

Maria rolled her eyes and Louie said mildly, "It's not a competition."

Beau scooped up his princess puppet and slipped her back into his coat pocket, while Maria snapped her fingers to dismiss the fire lion. Bess had nurtured a hope of taking one of the cobwebbed roses back with her for the Odditorium, but they were so delicate that the flowers were already falling apart in her hands. She let out a sigh as the sugary petals dusted the ground at her feet.

"The important thing is that we made it out of the caves," Louie said, sensing her disappointment.

"We'd all better keep an eye out for Easter eagles," Beau said. "Otherwise we might end up right back where we started in the mountains, getting pecked at by hungry eaglets."

Nobody wanted that so they all looked up at the sky. It was bright purple, just like yesterday, with the same fluffy black clouds. There was no sign of any eagles. For now.

"Cedric will look out for us," Maria said. Her little dragon was perched on her shoulder, staring intently up into the sky. "Now that he knows their scent, he'll tell me if they're coming."

"Good." Beau rubbed his hands together. "We've lost enough time. Let's push on to the Candymaker's mansion."

He took the map from his pocket and they crowded round it. "It's all the way over there." He pointed. "So it looks like the most direct route is to cross the fields and head through those graveyards."

"Are we sure we want to wander through a graveyard?" Louie asked. "It seems like they might be tricky places in the Land of Halloween Sweets."

"I don't think we have much choice," Bess said, studying the map. "There are rivers on either side and the ones I've seen so far all seem to be made from jelly. I don't think we'll be able to swim across very easily."

"Right then," Maria said, "graveyards it is."

ChAPTER 28

The children walked on, feeling glad to leave the eagle mountains behind them. They'd lost valuable time so they went as quickly as they could, stopping only at a stream for a drink. Bess had been right about the lack of water. Most of the streams appeared to be made from a sort of blue jelly, but they did find one that flowed with a fizzy bubblegum-flavoured liquid.

Before long, they reached their first graveyard. The tombstones were old and crumbling and they were also quite clearly made of chocolate. Many of them had fallen down altogether. You could still make out some of the names engraved on them though.

"Squidge Fudgehollow," Beau read as they passed by. "Peppersnap Snood. Flick Fizzbits. What kind of people have names like these?"

It was perfectly still and quiet in the graveyard. None of the graves had flowers on them. A couple of black liquorice flowers had sprung up through cracks in the pathway, but that was all.

"I saw some gummy worms popping out from one of the graves," Louie said. "But there don't seem to be many other signs of life here."

"Well, that's a good thing, I suppose," Beau said. "It means there's nothing to get in our way."

"Even if there's not much sign of life, there might still be some undead things lurking around," Bess pointed out. She was keeping her eyes peeled for gummy worms, wondering if they'd work for her flowers, but she hadn't seen any yet.

Beau frowned. "What a cheerful thought."

"She's right," Maria said. "This is a graveyard after all. We should tread carefully."

Just at that moment, the silence was broken by the sound of organ music spilling from the open door of a nearby church. It was a sad, eerie sort of tune – the kind of thing one might imagine unseen hands playing on pianos in the parlours of haunted houses. The children froze and looked at one another.

"We could skirt round the church?" Beau suggested. "We don't have to go inside."

"Perhaps we should try and make contact with the people of this land," Louie suggested. "Some of them might be friendly and even helpful. Like that witch fairy in the Forest of Chocolate Eyeballs."

Bess and Maria were undecided, but in the end it turned out they didn't have much choice. On one side of the church they were met by tall iron railings, and on the other side the way was choked by such a thick tangle of brambles that they would need an axe to hack their way through it.

"The lion could burn a path for us," Maria suggested. "But it might melt the chocolate tombstones nearby, which seems a bit disrespectful."

"Let's just try going through the church," Louie said. "We can't hide forever."

They doubled back round to the door and cautiously stepped inside. Even though it was old and disused, the church had a very similar smell to the one Bess knew back in Roseville. She breathed in cold old stones and snuffed-out candle smoke. It was quite a small building, and very much in need of a good clean, but the light still managed to shine through the stained-glass windows, painting rainbow colours upon the floor.

The pews were all empty. The prayer and hymn books were in an untidy jumble by the front door, with a couple of loose pages scattered here and there. The only sound was the music coming from the organ at the far end. It filled the large space, soaring all the way up to the high vaulted ceiling. The instrument was tucked round a corner so, although they could see its pipes reaching high, the children couldn't see who was playing it.

"Perhaps it's one of those automatic organs," Maria suggested. "There might be nobody there at all."

Bess hoped that wasn't the case. Now that they were here, she liked the thought of meeting another one of the land's inhabitants. Besides, the church didn't have a spooky feeling like she was expecting. It actually felt kind of nice. Slowly they began to make their way towards the front.

"Look at the pews," Bess whispered to the others.

"What about them?" Beau asked.

"They're really low to the ground," Bess said. "Whoever used to visit this church must have been quite short."

Indeed, the pews barely had any legs at all and were practically resting on the floor.

The children were almost at the organ now. They edged round some low benches that looked as if they might once have been used by a choir and then the bottom half of the organ finally came into view. It wasn't an automatic instrument after all – there was someone playing it. Just like the other seating in the church, the chair in front of the organ was set low to the ground. And the musician was a ghost.

ChapTeR 29

The ghostly organ-player was transparent enough for the children to see all the way through to the black and white keys on the other side. And not only was the musician a ghost – he was also very clearly a giant gummy bear. It looked as if he had once been a bright blue colour, but his ghostly transparency meant his original colours had faded. There were two little circular ears on top of his head and he had a large round tummy along with short stubby arms and legs. Bess could see the organ had been designed for gummy paws, with big keys within easy reach.

As the children approached, the ghostly gummy bear finished the song he was playing. He was about to launch straight into a new one, but then Louie cleared his throat.

"Um, hello," he said. "Please don't be alarmed – we're just visiting. That was a lovely song you just played."

The gummy bear swivelled round on his chair to look at them. The movement caused a faint smell of blueberry to waft through the air. Bess had never seen a gummy bear so large before and it was a little startling. He was easily as big as she was.

"Children!" the bear exclaimed in a high-pitched voice. "Children here again after all these years! Oh, if I could only..." He reached a paw out towards Louie, who was standing nearest to him. For a moment, it looked as if he was going to stroke his ear, but then the bear gave a sigh and his paw dropped to his side. "How did you get here? This world isn't safe. Not any more."

"What happened?" Beau asked.

"The Candymaker happened," the bear replied. "He moved in and his sweets gobbled up everything in their path. They even tore down the gummy queen's castle."

Bess thought of the crumbling pink castle she'd seen from the sky during the eagle flight.

"So...was this once some sort of land of gummy bears?" Maria asked.

"Yes," the bear squeaked. "We had villages, playgrounds, orchards and libraries. But the Halloween creatures only want haunted graveyards, bewitched forests and cursed mountains. There's hardly anything left of the gummy-bear world." The bear peered at them curiously. "Why would you come to a place like this?"

"We're looking for a ghostly gobstopper," Beau said. "We were told that the Candymaker has one."

"You'll never get into the Candymaker's mansion," the gummy bear said.

"Who *is* the Candymaker exactly?" Bess asked. "We keep hearing about him, but we don't really know who he is."

"I don't know much about him either," the bear replied. "Only that the gummy queen invited him here. She wanted him to make sweets for her Jubilee Picnic. It was meant to be a joyful celebration, but the Candymaker decided to take this world for himself instead."

"Can we speak to the queen?" Beau asked. "Does she haunt this church too?"

The bear shook his head. "Oh no, she haunts the ruins of her castle. I suggest you seek an audience with her though, if you truly mean to venture into the Candymaker's domain. She's the wisest of all the gummy bears and she'd want to know you're here and to see your lovely ears."

Beau frowned. "Pardon?"

"I mean, I know she'll want to help you if you're going to take a stand against the Candymaker. He ruined everything. He's the most evil person who ever existed and he has powerful magic too. Trust me, you'll need every bit of help you can get."

With that, the ghost bear vanished, leaving only his candy blueberry scent behind.

"Well, what now?" Maria said. Cedric was perched on her shoulder and snorted a puff of smoke. "Do we head straight to the mansion or go to see the queen first? The poor gummy bears. I wonder if there's anything we can do to help them?"

"Like what?" Beau asked. "I mean, they're all ghosts so they're pretty much beyond help, aren't they?"

"But they're haunting a world that's no longer their own," Louie pointed out. "Perhaps if we could remove the Candymaker somehow then we might make life – or the afterlife, I suppose – a bit easier for them."

"Let's not get up to any heroics," Beau said sternly. "We're here for the gobstopper, remember? Not to rescue ghostly gummy bears who never asked to be rescued in the first place. That bear seemed happy enough playing his organ, didn't he? I say we don't meddle. We grab the gobstopper and then get out before the gate closes. We need to focus on you, Louie. This is our one chance to help you fix your werewolf problem once and for all."

Bess wanted to do something for the gummy bears too, but it was hard to argue with Beau's logic. Even if they were willing to help, it seemed like it was too late for that now.

"The gummy queen's castle isn't too far from here," Bess said. "I saw it from the sky when the Easter eagles were flying over. Perhaps we should try to speak to her first. The Candymaker is obviously very dangerous and some extra knowledge might be the best weapon."

Beau took the map from his pocket. "You mean this castle here?" he said. "But it would still be a bit of a detour. I don't know if it's worth it. We might not even be able to find the gummy queen. Personally I'd prefer just to turn up at the mansion, dive in and take our chances."

"Of course you want to go diving in head first," Maria said. "That's what ninjas do. But I think Bess is right. We should try to find out what we're dealing with if we can."

"I agree," Louie said quietly.

Beau shrugged. "Then I'm outvoted," he said. "But, for the last time, I am *not* a ninja and I never went to ninja school. I don't think there's even such a thing as ninja school."

"That's exactly what a ninja would say," Maria replied with a grin.

Cedric puffed out an impatient little burst of flame then spread his spiny wings and took off from her shoulder towards the church's back door as if bored by the conversation.

The children followed the dragon out of the churchyard and on to the path on the other side. Now that they knew to look for it, they could see little signs of the old gummy-bear world here and there. Sometimes the dirt path gave way to pretty jewelled tiles made of boiled sweets. Or there'd be a bench with tiny legs. At one point, they even passed through what looked like the ruins of a gummy-bear village, with piles of straw and brick that had once been circular thatched cottages.

"That one's still standing – look," Maria said, pointing. "More or less."

When the children peeked through the windows, they saw a small living room with a low sofa, as well as a kitchen with pretty checked curtains at the windows and a pie dish on the window sill. It was empty of course, but perhaps a blueberry tart or apple pie had once been placed there to cool. In the garden, there were the remains of an old vegetable patch and a little pond with a duck house in the middle.

"It looks like this was a lovely place before the Candymaker came," Bess said sadly.

The children continued on their way, using Beau's map to ensure they were travelling in the right direction. After the gummy-bear village, they passed through another couple of graveyards and a giant pumpkin patch, where they stopped to eat some more candy beetles they found growing on a bush. Once again, Bess wondered whether the beetles might be suitable for her whispering flowers, but they showed no sign of being magical. The children picked a few more to take with them in case they got hungry later. After that, it was only a short walk down another jewelled path until they found themselves at the ruins of the gummy queen's castle.

ChaPTeR 30

The castle had once been a bright bubblegum pink, and the faint scent of candy still hung in the air, sweet and sugary. But now much of the building had crumbled away and there were dozens of black liquorice flowers growing through the gaps in the stones. The flowers had thick, thorny roots that had wrapped themselves all round the remains of the castle, causing it to collapse even further.

The sight reminded Bess of her whispering flowers back at the Odditorium, and she hoped that Jamie was managing to keep them under control and the exhibits safe. It looked as if there had once been a blue jelly moat surrounding the queen's castle, but this had mostly dried up, leaving behind only the sad skeletons of swans.

"The drawbridge is still intact," Bess pointed out. "So I guess we head in through there?"

The children walked slowly across the bridge. Everything felt unnaturally still and silent, and Bess couldn't shake the feeling that they were being watched, yet there didn't seem to be anyone around. When they passed beneath the drawbridge, they found some of the rooms in the castle lay in ruins, but others were very much intact, almost as if the gummy queen were about to return to them at any moment.

Strangely, there were lots of paintings of human ears hung about the place, along with a portrait hall containing paintings of past gummy-bear royalty. The bears looked much like the ghostly one they had met in the church, except that the royal bears all wore crowns. And they were a range of different colours too, from banana yellow to lime green. Beyond the portrait hall, they found a disused throne room with a sparkling gold throne at one end.

The children weren't able to explore the upper floors of the castle because the staircases had all collapsed and there seemed to be no sign of the gummy queen's ghost in the rooms they could get to. Bess was starting to worry that perhaps this visit would be a complete waste after all.

"Time to get out the ghost violin," Beau said, giving Louie a nudge. "She'll probably appear to hear your music. Ghosts can never resist the ghost violin, can they?"

They returned to the throne room, where Louie swung his violin case from his back and undid the clasps. He took out his white violin and began to play the same tune Bess had heard back on the train. As before, it was very beautiful and a bit eerie, and made the hairs on her arms stand on end. Bess held her breath, waiting for the arrival of the gummy queen.

She arrived on her throne halfway through Louie's tune. The queen's colour had faded into a ghostly shade, but it looked like she had once been a vivid royal purple and she still smelled faintly of gooseberries. There was a golden crown upon her head, nestled between her round ears, and she wore a luxurious fur-lined golden cape. She also had on a jewelled necklace that matched the sparkly sandals on her stubby feet.

When Louie finished and lowered his violin, the gummy queen applauded. It looked like an enthusiastic clap, but because her ghostly paws were made from jelly, the applause made a soft, squidgy sort of sound.

"Bravo, young man," the gummy queen said. "That was quite lovely."

Louie gave a bow. "Thank you, Your Majesty."

The gummy queen stood up. "I wouldn't normally allow wolves in the castle, however. Don't bother denying you're a werewolf – I can smell it on you. I hope your wolf side is quite under control?"

"Oh yes, Your Majesty," Louie hurried to assure her. "I only turn into a wolf during a full moon."

"Very good," the queen said. "I am Queen Lemony Pittipat the Third. Why are you here in my land? Or what *was* my land?"

"We've come to find a ghostly gobstopper," Maria said.

"Ah. You want to use it to stay in control as a werewolf?" the queen asked, looking at Louie.

"That's right," Beau said. "We've been told that the only one left is in the Candymaker's mansion. We've heard a lot about him, but we don't really know who he is or where he came from. Is there anything you can tell us that might help us in our quest?"

The gummy queen slowly shook her head. "I understand why you want the gobstopper," she said. "But you should give up any thought of going to the Candymaker's home. Once you set foot in there, you'll never come out."

"I wouldn't be so sure about that," Beau said. "You see, we're no ordinary children. You already know that

Louie's a werewolf. And that girl is a fire witch." He pointed at Maria, before moving his finger to Bess. "That one is a lock-picker. And I've got a puppet ninja mouse in my pocket. The Land of Halloween Sweets might seem tricksy to you, but some of us have been to places even more dangerous than this. Personally, I think that once you've survived the Land of Gruesome Hedgehogs, then you can survive anything."

The gummy queen regarded him curiously. "You only think that because you haven't yet met the Candymaker. He came from a land over the sea and his sweets were supposed to be the best in the world. He's no ordinary candymaker, you see, but a magician. One of his hands is made from candy and he has sugar eyes. I invited him here to spin sugar delights for my Jubilee Picnic more than a hundred years ago." She gave a sad little sniff.

"It was a beautiful day – the sky was blue and the sun was shining. The bunting was all hung up and the picnic blankets laid upon the lawn. But when the feast was unveiled the sweets all turned out to be horrible Halloween creatures who destroyed everything in their path. Our land was ruined in a matter of days. And now the Candymaker's magic has affected everything, even the weather. I still don't know why he did it."

"Didn't you have gummy-bear guards or anything like that?" Beau said. "Didn't anyone even try to stop him?"

"I had no guards," the queen said. "There was no need. We never had any trouble here. Everything was perfect until the Candymaker came. If you've got any sense, then you'll go back home at once." She paused, looking suddenly thoughtful. "But I can see that you're all unusually brave children. And you have lovely ears, quite lovely. I'd hate for anything to happen to them. So, if you're *really* set on venturing into the mansion, then you should try to find the sugar gummy-bear sweet and destroy it."

"Why?" Louie asked.

"That sweet is the source of all the Candymaker's power," the gummy queen said. "It's made entirely from sugar with a little red heart inside. Destroy it and you might just have a chance of escaping this land with your lives."

"How do we do that?" Bess said.

"It needs to be submerged in water," the queen replied. "That's the only way."

"Thank you, Your Majesty," Beau said. "That's really useful to know."

"Oh, and one other thing," the queen said. "You seem like nice enough children so, before you go, perhaps you might do me a favour and release Flossie from the caves?"

"Flossie?" Maria repeated. "Who's that?"

"My pet dragon," the gummy queen said. "Dragons live for a long time, so Flossie is still there in the caves beneath the castle, but she's old now and terribly lonely. A ghost owner is a poor substitute for a living one. I can't stroke her, you see, and that's what pets need most of all. It's a very sad thing for a sweet old dragon to live out her final days by herself."

Louie looked appalled. "Oh, how terrible. No pet should end up alone."

"You're a kind boy," the queen said. "I knew you would help. Here's the key." She pressed a button in the arm of the throne and a hidden compartment emerged containing a shining key. "It opens a door in the cave wall that will allow her to fly away and live out her remaining time in the mountains."

Beau stared at the key, looking suddenly suspicious. "But why was the dragon locked up in the caves in the first place if she's your pet?"

"The Candymaker wanted to add her to his collection," the queen said. "I doubt he'll be much interested in her any more though. She's too old and past her prime. She'll head straight for the mountains so she won't be in any danger. I'd have released her myself, but the cave door is too heavy for a ghost to force open. Thank you, children. I'm most grateful."

Before anyone could say anything else, the gummy queen disappeared. Louie took the key from the throne and Beau frowned at him.

"Don't even think about it," he said. "We are *not* here to rescue an elderly gummy dragon. We are absolutely, definitely not doing it. Now come on – let's get out of here."

ChAPTER 31

A short while later, the children had located the entrance to the castle caves and were making their way down a winding stone staircase. There were torches on the walls, but they had all long since blown out, so Maria conjured her fire lion to lead the way and provide them with light. Beau was keeping up a constant muttering stream of complaints, making it very clear that he didn't want to waste time doing this.

"You can go ahead if you want to," Louie said mildly. "But if there's an old lonely pet here that needs freeing then I'm not leaving without it."

Maria seemed a little exasperated by their rescue mission too, but she just said that the sooner they got on with it, the sooner they could leave. As for Bess, she was thrilled at the thought of exploring the caves and seeing another dragon. And she liked Louie even more for the fact that he wanted to help the creature.

"I'd want someone to help Blizzard if they could," she said, feeling a sudden longing to see the old alligator.

"Cedric might quite like to meet another dragon," Maria added. "If he wakes up in time." The little lump in her T-shirt pocket and the snoring sounds told them that Cedric was currently snoozing in there.

"Look!" Bess said. "There's light up ahead."

They'd reached the final step and went through a low archway to find themselves in a cave. The walls were sparkling with gummy glow-worms and fireflies, lit up like hundreds of tiny torches. The children no longer needed the fire lion to see by so Maria clicked her fingers and he faded away.

The cave was very big. Rock pools glistened between the stalagmites and stalactites and it was stuffed full with jewels of every kind. There were pink diamonds and blue sapphires, red rubies and huge white pearls. Only they weren't precious stones, but made from candy instead. The smell was so sweet in the air that it was like they were breathing in sugar.

And there in the middle of the cave, fast asleep on a huge mound of candy rubies, was the largest sweet of all. Flossie was huge – a bright pink colour with just a touch of grey around her long snout to give away the fact that she was old. Her spiny wings were curled round her body and her long ridged tail was tucked beneath her. Even though she was made of candy and the queen had assured them she was a sweet old pet, it was hard not to feel a little bit nervous around an animal so big.

"The queen never mentioned what her dragon eats, did she?" Beau whispered. "For all we know, it's children."

The dragon must have had good hearing in spite of her age, because she immediately opened her eyes. Bess saw that they were a deep emerald green. The dragon blinked a few times in a sleepy sort of way before lifting her huge head and gazing down at them. The children took a nervous step back and Beau quickly reached for his ninja mouse. As soon as the puppet landed on the floor, it brandished its axe at the dragon, but Flossie only gave a low grunting rumble of pleasure and then breathed out a spray of bubbles over them.

"I don't think she's about to gobble us all up," Maria said.

Inside her pocket, Cedric woke up at the sound of another dragon and scrambled out to fly over. He landed on Flossie's snout, peering up at her curiously. There was a bit of grunting back and forth as they had some kind of dragon conversation, and then Cedric swooped back to Maria's shoulder.

"Cedric likes her, so I reckon she's safe," Maria said.

It was obvious Flossie was friendly just by looking at her. Not only was she still happily breathing bubbles over them, but she had a sweet, dopey face that reminded Bess of the cows in Roseville's fields. Candy jewels tumbled over themselves as Flossie carefully picked her way across to the children, laying her big head on the ground at their feet. Louie reached out to give her snout a rub and she made a purring sort of sound.

"Well, we've managed to find her," Beau said, stuffing the ninja mouse back in his pocket. "Now what? Where's this door out of the caves?"

"It's over there." Bess pointed to a massive door. It seemed to be made from a huge slab of shiny toffee.

Louie quickly went over to unlock it. It was so sticky that all the children had to throw their weight against it to force it open. Sunlight spilled inside and they all expected Flossie to fly out at once and soar straight to the mountains. But instead she looked right at them, then pointed to her own back with one of her jelly claws.

Louie turned to the others. "I think she wants us to climb on."

Chapter 32

Bess wasn't sure how she would manage to climb on to the dragon's back at first, but it turned out to be simpler than she'd expected. Flossie had gummy scales and these were easy enough to grip and use as hand- and footholds. In a matter of moments, all four children were nestled in a row right between her shoulder blades. Louie was perched at the front, followed by Beau, Bess and Maria.

As soon as they were settled and holding on tightly, Flossie launched off the ground, flapping her huge wings, and they were flying towards the open door. Bess couldn't help ducking low to the dragon's back, worried that Flossie might misjudge the gaps between the stalactites. But she swooped around them quite elegantly, taking them straight out the doorway. They flew out into the castle grounds, over the ruins of a rose garden, and then the dragon soared up into the sky.

The sun had disappeared behind a cloud while they'd been inside the caves. The sky had turned dark blue and looked as if it was going to rain soon. Nevertheless, Bess found this flight far more enjoyable than the one with the Easter eagles. It was as if Flossie knew where they wanted to go because the mansion in the distance got closer and closer as she soared straight over a series of graveyards.

"I'm not sure Flossie should get much closer to the Candymaker's home," Louie said, glancing back at the others. "What if he decides to try to collect her after all?"

"But we're so close!" Beau groaned. "And this world's gate will close soon. I think we should—"

Just then the clouds above them broke – and it turned out that they didn't contain rain. Instead, gummy frogs started to pour down from the sky. They were about the size of normal frogs, but made from gummy candy in a variety of colours. They splatted and squelched on the children in a most revolting way. It seemed that the dragon didn't like flying through frogs either because she quickly swooped down to the ground.

The children found themselves surrounded by vegetable patches. Bess thought this was one of the most orderly parts of the world she'd seen so far. Everything was very tidy and lined up in neat rows. She was surprised to see vegetables in a land of sweets, but there was no time for them to examine their surroundings properly because they needed to escape the falling frogs. Bess didn't usually mind frogs, but there was something a bit unpleasant about having a heavy, wet one slipping around on your head. As Bess swept a frog from her hair, she guessed they would count as magic food for her whispering flowers, but she couldn't possibly think of feeding them to the flowers if they were alive.

"Look, there's a bandstand just over there." Beau pointed. "Let's take cover."

The children quickly said goodbye to Flossie and the dragon lumbered off, presumably to get clear of the frog rain and then head to the mountains. Bess and the others ran through the falling frogs, past a couple of bedraggled scarecrows to the bandstand in the middle of the vegetable patches.

"If the rain here is made of gummy frogs, then I'd hate to know what happens when it snows," Beau said, peering out at the spectacle.

"Or when there's a tornado or hurricane," Louie added. "The gummy queen said the Candymaker's magic affected the weather, didn't she? I wonder if he's doing this on purpose? Perhaps he knows we're here and is trying to slow us down."

"How long do you think the frog rain will last?" Maria said. "We can't afford to wait too long."

"The gate doesn't close until sunset tomorrow," Louie pointed out. "We should have time."

"As long as we get a move on," Beau grumbled. "No more silly sidetracking."

"We're almost there," Bess said. "The Candymaker's mansion is just on the other side of this vegetable patch. We can walk to it from here once the rain stops."

Beau took the map from his pocket and examined it. "Professor Ash might beat us to it at this rate," he said. "It looks like he'll have had to journey about the same distance from the Forest of Chocolate Eyeballs. I can't see any train routes that will have helped so he's probably had to go on foot. I guess it depends on how many pitfalls and perils he's come across."

Bess gazed out through the falling frogs. They were coming down thick and fast now and she was glad the four of them were no longer in the air. There was no sign of Flossie, and Bess hoped the dragon was already well on her way to the mountains.

"This seems like a strange sort of place for a bandstand," Bess remarked as she turned back to the others.

Roseville had a bandstand in the middle of the rose garden and musicians often played there during the town's musical evenings. Bess had never heard of musical evenings happening in a vegetable patch before though.

"Come to think of it, the Land of Halloween Sweets seems like an odd place to find vegetable patches," Beau said. "What do you think they're growing?"

None of them knew, but it seemed unlikely to be carrots and turnips. After a short while, the frogs stopped falling from the sky and were replaced with candy tadpoles, which wiggled their way into the ground like worms when they landed. After the tadpoles, some jelly frogspawn fell down in wet splats until, at last, the clouds parted and the sun shone down once again.

"About time," Beau said. "Let's get this show on the road."

They picked their way through the melting frogspawn and down a narrow path between vegetable patches.

Before long, they realised that they weren't actually vegetable patches at all, but big beds of herbs.

"The signs say which herb it is," Louie said. "It looks like they're all types of mint."

Now that he mentioned it, Bess noticed the smell of mint in the air, along with cocoa from the chocolate soil.

"So nothing to do with Halloween or sweets at all then?" Maria said, crouching down to take a closer look at the nearest cluster of herbs.

"Perhaps it's left over from the gummy-bear world?" Beau suggested.

Bess shook her head as she read the signs. "My mum has a herb garden. She grows banana mint and spearmint, but I've never heard of mummy mint and I've *definitely* never heard of Frankenmint."

"Hmm, now that you mention it, neither have I," Beau said.

"It's too bad there aren't any carrots," Maria said. "I'm getting a bit sick of having sweets for breakfast, lunch and dinner. And check it out – the leaves of this one really do look like a carrot. Perhaps a vegetable slipped in by accident?"

Bess thought that this was just wishful thinking on Maria's part – the leaves seemed exactly like those of a mint plant to her. But, before she could say anything, Maria had gripped the plant by the stem and yanked it out of the chocolate soil.

What absolutely nobody was expecting to see was a furious miniature mummy, his white bandages covered in smears of chocolate soil, his little hands clenched into fists as he thrashed and kicked and grumbled in Maria's grasp.

Chapter 33

Maria let out a yelp of surprise. She dropped the minty mummy on to the ground, where he lurched about in a disoriented circle, his arms stuck straight out in front of him. He looked just like a classic mummy except for the cluster of mint leaves growing out of the top of his bandaged head – and the fact that he was only about thirty centimetres tall.

"What even is that thing?" Maria gasped, watching the mummy as he staggered to and fro. "Is he made from mint? Is he a sweet? I can't tell!"

"Why don't you lick him and find out?" Beau suggested sarcastically. "And why did you pull him up from the ground in the first place? Any one of us could have told you that that plant wasn't a carrot!"

"How was I supposed to know there was a bandaged-up mummy hidden in the soil?" Maria snapped back. "No one could have guessed that!"

"Well, we're in the Land of Halloween Sweets," Beau pointed out. "We have to expect the unexpected."

"It doesn't matter," Louie said soothingly. "There's no harm done—"

But that was as far as he got before the mummy's grasping hands came into contact with two more mint plants. He grabbed and yanked, bringing a couple more mummies up from the soil. Bess suddenly remembered what her mum had told her about how sturdy and resilient mint plants were and realised that this might be a trickier problem to sort out than they'd first thought.

"That doesn't look good," Beau groaned. "Quick, let's put them back!"

He lunged for the nearest mummy, but it was too late. The other two had already lurched to their feet and pulled up the buried mummies beside them. In a matter of minutes, there were dozens of minty mummies shuffling around. Not only that, but they freed some of the Frankenmint too. These looked just like little Frankenstein's monsters with square heads, green skin and bolts through their necks. They were about the same size as the mummies and also had sprigs of mint sprouting from the tops of their blocky heads. Bess felt quite alarmed by the sheer number of monsters swarming the ground at their feet. They may have been small, but there were loads of them.

"I think we'd better leave," Louie said quietly. "It's too late to put them back. Hopefully the gardeners – whoever they are – won't be too annoyed. I think we should go before the minty monsters turn their attention to us."

They set off down the nearest path. At the end of it was a gate leading out of the herb garden, but before they could reach it a swarm of minty mummies blocked the way. Their bright, beady black eyes peered out at the children from beneath the bandages and they froze.

"What do you think they want?" Maria asked nervously.

"To eat our brains probably," Beau sighed. "That's a mummy thing, isn't it?" He looked at Maria. "You'd best get your fire lion ready. My ninja mouse is good, but I don't think he can take on all of them without backup."

"Hold your horses," Louie said softly. "They might not mean us any harm at all." Before anyone could stop him, he took a step forward on the path and crouched down to the mummies' level. "Hello," he said. "I'm Louie Ash and it's a pleasure to meet you. I'm terribly sorry about the mix-up. We just thought one of you might be a carrot and—"

"How *dare* you disturb our slumber!" one of the mummies hissed through its bandages.

"To be fair, we only disturbed *one* of your slumbers," Beau said, stepping to Louie's side. "And that mummy disturbed the rest of you."

"How *dare* you disturb our slumber!" the mummy snarled again, sounding even crosser.

One by one, the other mummies began repeating this phrase in their scratchy little voices and then they were all lurching forward, their tiny bandaged hands stretched out towards the children.

Beau tugged Louie to his feet and the four of them ran back down the path the way they'd come, only to find a second group of minty mummies there, muttering furiously. They were trapped.

"I know," Bess said, shrugging off her backpack. "Perhaps they'd like some apple blossom as a peace offering."

"But didn't you say the apples were poisonous?" Louie said, sounding worried.

"Yes, but there are different types of poisoned apple," Bess said. "These ones just make people tell the truth and the blossom gives you knowledge. They're really interesting facts normally too. Here, look."

She brought out the book and opened it. The apple tree unfolded from its pages and Bess was pleased to see that there was even more blossom than the last time she'd looked.

She quickly plucked a few petals from the tree and scattered them over the heads of the mummies, filling the air with the fresh scent of apples. Immediately, the minty mummies stopped their grumbling and began sniffing the air instead.

Bess knew that various fascinating facts would be popping into their heads and this certainly seemed to be doing a good job of distracting them. They weren't reaching out towards the children any more, but were staring into space with a glazed look instead. Perhaps they were mulling over the fact that a slug has four noses or that an owl can't move its eyes. Bess quietly closed the book to fold up the tree and tucked the whole thing back into her bag.

The children were just about to start tiptoeing past the mummies when a voice rang out behind them.

"Oh, for goodness' sake, what's going on here? Those mummies aren't ready to be picked yet! And the Frankenmint is only meant to be harvested under a full moon. The sun dazzles them!"

Bess saw that the handful of Frankenmints were, indeed, squinting in a blinded sort of way. She turned round to see who had told them off and found herself face to face with a cross-looking gnome.

Bess couldn't help staring. Being from Roseville, she had seen many ornamental garden gnomes of course. There were dozens of the little statues in the rose garden, with pointed red hats, smart green jackets and shiny shoes. They were usually shown digging or fishing or perhaps relaxing in a deckchair. But the one before her was a Halloween gnome. He had an orange hat covered in printed bats and his jacket and trousers were black and stitched with silver stars. There were tiny plastic spiders caught up in his long silver beard and his black shoes curled up at the toes like a Christmas elf's, only they had little grinning pumpkins dangling from the ends rather than bells.

"It'll take me ages to get them all put back where they were," the gardener gnome went on with a sigh.

Now that the scent of apple blossom had faded away, the creatures went back to stumbling around, grumbling and muttering. The gnome scrabbled in his pocket and tossed some tiny pairs of sunglasses over to the Frankenmints. Once these were on, the little monsters settled down and were less flappy. The mummies were still quite feisty though, creeping closer to the children with their muttered complaints of, "How *dare* you disturb our slumber!"

The gnome whipped out a plant mister and sprayed a few droplets of water over them. The mummies instantly shrank back with little gasps of horror.

"We're very sorry, sir," Louie began. "It was an accident—"

"An accident? How do you accidentally pick a mummy?" the gnome replied, rolling his eyes. "I haven't even got my ghost orchestra here today and that's the only way to tuck them back up in the soil where they belong. They're all supposed to be sleeping right now, and a lullaby is the one thing that settles them." He gave the children a sharp look. "Can any of you lot whistle?"

"I have a ghost violin," Louie offered. "I could play a lullaby for them?"

"Ghost violin, eh?" The gnome gave him a doubtful look. "All right, give it a try."

Louie hastily removed his violin from its case and began to play a sweet, lilting lullaby. The mummies and Frankenmints began stretching and yawning and the next moment they were traipsing back to the holes in the chocolate soil.

The gardener gnome still seemed quite irritated about it all though. "Is it really so much to ask to be able to grow my minty monsters in peace?"

"But… But why are you growing minty monsters in the first place?" Beau asked. "What are they *for*?"

"What kind of question is that?" the gnome snapped. "Why does anyone grow anything? It makes more sense than growing turnips or something like that, doesn't it?"

"Well…not really," Bess said. "I mean, turnips don't taste very nice, but at least you can put them in a soup. But I *definitely* think these little mummies are cooler than turnips," she hurried to add.

"And things don't always have to be useful, do they? Sometimes it's enough to be unique and weird and wonderful."

"Well, I'm glad you think so, but you've completely ruined this one," the gnome said, gesturing at one of the mummies. "Look, the lullaby isn't working on him. I guess he was the first one you picked? He's been out of the soil too long and now that he won't get back in it he's no use to me at all. I'll have to throw him on the compost heap."

"Oh, could I take him instead?" Bess suggested eagerly.

A miniature minty mummy would definitely be the sort of thing to draw in new visitors to the Odditorium. She guessed he'd probably count as magic food for the flowers too, but there was no way she could think of feeding him to them. It was the same problem as with the frogs – anything sentient felt too cruel. She was seriously beginning to worry whether she would find anything that could help save the Odditorium in this land. Her heart gave an anxious little flutter at the thought of the museum being overrun with whispering flowers.

The gnome shrugged. "Be my guest. He'll never get any bigger though."

The gnome handed the mummy over to Bess, along with a small coffin-shaped box. "He'll sleep well enough if you put him in there."

"Thanks." Bess removed the lid from the coffin. The mummy climbed in and went straight to sleep, making contented little snoring noises. "Is there anything else I need to know about how to look after him?" she asked. "Does he…I don't know, need food or anything like that?"

The gnome looked surprised. "Food? He's a minty mummy. Of course he doesn't need food! He just needs a comfortable coffin to sleep in and a dark place to prowl around when he's awake."

Bess thanked the gnome again and carefully placed the mummy in her bag.

Louie finished his lullaby now that all the other monsters were back in their holes. The children then helped to cover them up with chocolate soil so that only their leaves poked through again. Finally, the herb garden looked perfectly quiet and ordinary, apart from the fact that they could faintly hear a muffled "How *dare* you disturb our slumber!" as a couple of mummies muttered to themselves in their sleep.

Bess longed to find out more about the little monsters, but the gardener gnome was clearly not in a chatty mood. When Maria tried to ask him whether he knew anything about the Candymaker, the gnome shook his head. "The Candymaker likes to be left alone and so do I. Now scat!" he said, squirting them with water from his bottle. "Before I set the scarecrows on you."

The children apologised again as they hurried away from his herb garden.

ChaPTeR 34

"It looks like we're running out of daylight," Beau said, pointing up at the sky.

He was right. The light was fading as dusk swept in.

"I still think it might be better if we don't wait until the morning to go into the mansion," Beau went on. "I could probably be in and out within the hour—"

"Absolutely not!" Louie said at once. "Going into a villain's mansion by yourself at night is an amateur thing to do, even if you are a ninja. We don't want you to get chained up in a dungeon or sucked into a cursed painting or something. We go in together or not at all. We have time before the gate closes tomorrow."

Bess hoped he was right, but she felt worried. Not only would the gate back to their world be closing soon, but she still needed to find food for the whispering flowers.

Louie pulled out his pocket watch and opened the case. "It's going to be a full moon again tonight so I think I've only got a few more minutes before I turn into a wolf. *Promise* you won't go into the mansion without me."

Beau grumbled, but reluctantly gave his promise. The children just about had time to walk the rest of the way to the Candymaker's house before the sun began to sink through the sky, moving every bit as quickly as it had the day before. Great clouds of candy bats swooped through the air once again as the sunset painted the sky pink and red.

"See you in the morning!" Louie said hurriedly before running off into a nearby forest.

The sun disappeared and the full moon swiftly rose in its place. A short distance away, they heard the howl of a wolf. Bess couldn't help shivering a little. It was such a mournful sound, but somehow dangerous too, warning people to stay away. Beau took his wolf-whisperer puppet from his pocket and set him down on the ground.

"The puppet will warn us if Louie comes back," he said. "Now we'd better find somewhere to set up camp. How about the forest?"

Although they knew Louie was in there somewhere, it looked as if the forest would be big enough for all of them and they could stay hidden from the Candymaker. But as soon as they stepped inside, they realised that it wasn't really a forest at all. What Bess had assumed were trees were actually tall towers of pumpkins. And the orange light she'd thought was from the moon was instead spilling from their grinning faces.

Most of the pumpkins were orange, but some were more unusual colours – black, silver, white or red. Leaves and vines spilled out between and around the pumpkins, which was partly what had fooled them all into thinking this was a forest. Bess noticed that there were small silver charms hanging from some of the leaves, shining in the pumpkin light.

"What is this place?" Beau said, squinting up at the pumpkins. He pulled the map from his pocket and stared at it for a moment. Then he turned the piece of paper upside down. "Ah, we're on the other side of the mansion from the one I thought." He held the paper out for the girls to see and pointed at the map. "So I thought we were here, in the Forest of Marshmallow Ghosts, but we're actually in the Fairy Godmother's Pumpkin Patch."

Maria shrugged. "Well, a fairy godmother is probably better than marshmallow ghosts anyway."

Bess frowned at the map. Something didn't quite feel right. "Why would a fairy godmother be here in the Land of Halloween Sweets?" she asked. "Surely she should be in the Land of Fairy Tales or something?"

"Well, the Easter eagles aren't originally from here either," Maria pointed out. "And I guess the godmothers need a lot of space to grow their pumpkins. They turn into carriages, don't they? In the stories."

Bess thought back to the story of Cinderella in her book of fairy tales. "Yes, but I'm pretty sure that Cinderella's pumpkin wasn't a jack-o'-lantern," she said. "It didn't have a grinning, evil-looking face in any of the pictures."

"Either way, we're here now," Beau said. "I vote we just make camp. We don't want to be wandering around half the night, and if we go off somewhere else then it'll make it harder for Louie to find us in the morning. Let's just all make a pact that we won't disturb any of the pumpkins." He gave Maria a stern look. "We don't want a repeat of the minty mummies. If we leave her pumpkins alone, then hopefully the fairy godmother will leave us alone too."

They all agreed this was a sensible idea, so they found a clearing between some pumpkin towers and set about making themselves comfortable. Maria put a fire fence up round them, in case Louie should return, then they took out some of the candy beetles they'd collected earlier and had them for dinner. Bess couldn't help thinking Maria was right and that sweets for every meal was starting to get a bit tedious. She would have really liked a nice hot bowl of her dad's vegetable soup just then.

"I hope those pumpkin towers are stable," Beau said, gazing up at them. "There must be twenty pumpkins or more stacked on top of each other. They seem a bit wobbly, don't they?"

Bess looked up at the nearest tower. It was the only one inside the fire fence and the pumpkins were all grinning down in a watchful sort of way. Most of them were orange, but then Bess's eyes fell on a green one and she couldn't stop staring at it. There was something different about it, something special, something wonderful. It was the most stunning emerald green and it seemed to be looking right at Bess, like it recognised her. Not only that, but Bess had the feeling that the pumpkin had been waiting for her too.

She glanced at the other two to see if they were experiencing something similar, but they were both eating their candy beetles and discussing how to get into the Candymaker's mansion. Bess looked back at the emerald pumpkin. She felt a great longing to touch it, as if it were a magnet drawing her in. Before she knew what was happening, she had stood up.

"Where are you off to?" Beau asked.

"I just… I really want to take a look at that green pumpkin," Bess replied. "I promise I won't touch it."

The pumpkin's grinning smile seemed to pull her in as she walked closer. It was the fifth pumpkin in the tower, which put it at about Bess's height. She stopped directly in front of it and as she looked at the pumpkin she felt something tingle in the air between them like an electric current. Her breath caught in her throat and the hairs on her arms stood on end. It could only be magic making the air fizz like that.

Her fingers ached to reach out and touch the pumpkin, but she kept her hands firmly clenched by her sides. It didn't matter though because, without warning, the emerald pumpkin jumped into her arms. The movement caused the entire tower to collapse and suddenly there were pumpkins rolling and bumping round them in all directions.

ChAPTeR 35

Maria and Beau both leaped to their feet and the three children looked on in horror at the mess around them. Not only had the pumpkin tower toppled over, but something was happening to the emerald pumpkin in Bess's hands. It was growing before their eyes. Within seconds, it was so big that Bess had to put it down on the ground. And it wasn't just growing, it was changing shape too until it had wheels and a door. Finally, it wasn't a pumpkin any more at all but a carriage. A magnificent, gleaming green carriage.

Beau groaned. "You *promised* you wouldn't touch it!"

"I swear I didn't!" Bess said. "The pumpkin... I know it sounds crazy, but it jumped at me!"

They all stared at the carriage. Bess thought it was fantastically beautiful. It was the same emerald green colour as the pumpkin had been, with big looping twists of black iron curling above and round the wheels. But this was no Cinderella's carriage. It didn't glitter or sparkle. Instead, it glowed in the firelight in a powerful, malevolent sort of way. And when Bess peered inside she saw that the velvet seating within was a dark purple colour. An inky black crow formed a crest over the door. These were, quite clearly, a villain's colours.

"I don't think the fairy godmother is going to be very happy about this," Beau said, glancing round the clearing.

Right on cue, the fairy godmother herself suddenly appeared beside them in a puff of purple smoke. She was human-sized, but she definitely wasn't a kindly, grandmotherly type like the godmother in Bess's book. This pale woman was young and beautiful, but she also looked every inch the bad fairy. Her dress was long and laced and black as midnight. Her fairy ears were pointed, her lipstick was blood-red and so were her nails. Ruby jewels glittered in her dark hair and on her long fingers. She also seemed extremely annoyed.

Maria conjured her fire lion, but the big cat only managed to bare its teeth for a moment before the fairy snapped her fingers and turned him into a little fire kitten.

"Hey!" Maria protested as the kitten gave a feeble, indignant meow at her feet. "What did you do to my lion?"

"Oh, he'll be back to his usual shape in an hour or two," the fairy replied with a wave of her hand. "Now which one of you picked the pumpkin?"

Bess stepped forward. "I'm very sorry," she began. "It jumped into my arms and—"

But the fairy cut her off. "You young people are all so impatient these days!" she said. "I'd have come to you if you'd only given me half a chance. There's really no need to trespass on my patch to pick your own pumpkin, but you're here now so we may as well get on with it. Which one are you then? An evil queen or a wicked stepsister?"

"What? Oh, I'm… I'm not," Bess stuttered. "I'm neither of those things. I'm just…ordinary."

"Not a chance!" the fairy godmother snorted. "You must have evil queen or wicked stepsister blood in you somewhere. Otherwise the pumpkin wouldn't work."

"*Are* you a fairy godmother then?" Beau asked dubiously. "It's just that you look more like a bad fairy or a wicked witch or something. No offence," he added hurriedly.

The fairy gave an elegant shrug. "What makes you think that I can't be a bad fairy *and* a fairy godmother? And who decides what's good or bad anyway? I prefer the moon to sunlight and I like bats better than fluffy kittens. I also prefer cursed and interesting things to rainbows, but does that make me bad?"

Bess stayed quiet. She preferred all those things herself.

"There's room for all types of people in this world," the fairy said. "And it seems like you children should know that better than anyone." She glanced at the wolf-whisperer puppet still patrolling the perimeter. "Oh yes, I can see it on you all – your powers. But anyway back to business," she went on briskly. "My name is Ember." She snapped her fingers at Maria. "You there. Try picking a pumpkin."

Maria obediently did as she was asked and reached down for a little white pumpkin on the ground by her feet. But, when she picked it up, nothing happened. There was no transformation, no carriage. Just a plain, ordinary pumpkin in her hands.

"You see?" Ember said, looking at Bess. "Nothing happened when your friend did it because she doesn't have any wicked stepsister or evil queen blood in her. *You,* on the other hand, most certainly do or else you wouldn't have a carriage. Let's take a look at it then."

Ember walked round the emerald carriage, inspecting it closely. "Hmm," she said at last. "Looks like one from the wicked stepsister range. You see, there's no crown painted here on the door and there would be if this was a queen's carriage. Still, I always thought the stepsisters were far more interesting, personally. Some of them went on to do truly astonishing things. Such vision. One can't help but admire them." She peered closely at Bess. "Are you really saying you had no idea?"

"No." Bess shook her head. "I didn't."

And yet...perhaps it made sense? Maybe this was why she had always felt so different from everybody else. Maybe this was why she was strange and liked strange things. Maybe it was the reason Echo had let Bess stroke her and the reason she'd been able to press a poisoned-apple tree. She could feel herself squirming a little and glanced at Maria and Beau, worried about what they might think. After all, if Bess were descended from a wicked stepsister, then surely that must make her bad too? She wondered if Pops had known.

"I don't feel wicked," she blurted out. "I know I'm a bit different and like odd things, but—"

Ember snorted. "Well, perhaps the word 'wicked' just got used by lazy and ignorant people to describe something they couldn't understand. As I just said, good and bad are a matter of perspective. Sometimes people say wicked when they actually mean powerful or ambitious or unique. That isn't to say that the stepsisters weren't also dangerous of course. Or that they didn't have darkness. But I rather think that's what made them special. I only provide the raven, by the way, not the horse." She tapped the carriage. "You'll have to transform your own mouse for that."

"I could make you a fire horse," Maria suggested, looking quite excited by the prospect.

Ember gave her an approving look. "Now you're talking."

"I'm sorry, what was that about a raven?" Bess asked. She peered in through the carriage windows and thought she glimpsed the sleek gleam of dark feathers.

"Your raven companion," Ember replied. She looked surprised by Bess's ignorance and gave a sigh. "Look, this is how it works. Princesses get a carriage, a ballgown and a pair of magic slippers. Wicked stepsisters get a carriage, a raven and a book. I'm sure you'll figure it all out. The book will help."

She snapped her fingers and the carriage immediately shrank back into a pumpkin. Then she produced a black silk bag from one of her dress pockets and slipped the pumpkin inside. She handed it to Bess. "If you touch it with your bare hands, then it will turn into a carriage. If you want it to go back to being a pumpkin, then just whisper that it's midnight. It doesn't matter if it actually is midnight or not. The pumpkin won't know the difference."

"Thanks," Bess said, accepting the bag a little uncertainly.

"You may stay here for the night, but perhaps you'd be so kind as to remove yourselves in the morning," Ember said. "The pumpkins get excitable when there are visitors around." She glanced at Maria. "And fire witches make them especially nervous."

"We'll be gone," Beau said. "Would you like us to try to stack the pumpkins up again?"

"Thank you, but no," Ember said. "Best leave them where they are. And now I'll bid you goodnight." She flashed them a sudden smile. "Don't let the candy bats bite."

She disappeared in another puff of purple smoke.

Bess looked at the others but, to her relief, they seemed quite unfazed by the revelation about her heritage and were more interested in the carriage.

"It'll make a great means of transport in magical lands if we have to leave the train again," Beau said. "Between Maria's fire horse and your pumpkin, we'll be able to cover ground much more quickly."

"I'm not going on other adventures with you after this though," Bess pointed out reluctantly. "It's just this one."

Beau and Maria fell silent.

"I forgot," said Beau.

"So did I," Maria added.

"It just…seems like you're one of the team now," Beau went on. "It's weird to think you won't come with us next time."

Bess felt a flutter of pleasure in her belly at his words.

"I would so love to come," she said. "But I have my normal life at home and school. The magic scarecrow can't cover for me in class forever."

"Why don't you run away?" Beau suggested. "That's what I did. Just leave it all behind and join the train for good."

It was a tempting idea, but Bess shook her head. "I couldn't do that to my parents. They'd be so sad. And I wouldn't want to leave the Odditorium forever."

The children fell silent again. Finally, Maria said, "We'll think of something. But right now I reckon we should all get some sleep. We want to be as ready as we can for the Candymaker's mansion tomorrow. Unless you want to take another look at the carriage? I imagine you're desperate to see inside it."

Bess shook her head. "I think I'd rather do that later."

Part of her was burning with curiosity, but the other part felt a little unsure and her mind was a whirl. She needed to let everything settle before finding out any more. So the children made themselves comfortable for the night. As Bess put down her bag to use as a pillow, she could feel the weight of the pumpkin and felt a confusing mix of concern, excitement and warmth towards her new friends – as well as hope for whatever the future might bring.

CHAPTER 36

Louie found them in the pumpkin patch the next morning. Apart from a few twigs and leaves still stuck in his hair, there was no outward sign that he'd spent the night as a wolf. His clothes had mended themselves as before and once he tidied up his hair he looked back to normal. Like the other two, he seemed unconcerned by the discovery that Bess was descended from a wicked stepsister.

"I thought you might mind," Bess said uncertainly. "All of you."

Louie looked surprised. "Why?"

"Well…because a wicked stepsister is a villain. That's what everyone thinks."

"People think werewolves are villains too," Louie said.

"And witches," Maria piped up.

"I don't think people usually have an opinion on puppeteers one way or another," Beau mused. "But most people would think we should be looking for a means to cure Louie of being a werewolf altogether rather than only helping him control it."

Bess hadn't thought about that. "Is there a way to stop being a werewolf?"

"I'm not sure," Louie said. "But I don't really want to stop. Being a werewolf, I mean. A wolf isn't good or bad – it's just a wolf. And I like the feeling of the wind in my fur when I run around in the moonlight. In fact, there's lots of stuff I like about being a wolf. It's part of who I am now. I just want to be able to control it, that's all."

It made sense to Bess. If she had the power to turn into a wolf, she wasn't sure she'd want to give that up either. The children walked on in thoughtful silence, following the path. Bess was just wishing that Pops were still alive to talk to about all this when Louie fell into step beside her.

"I think it's really cool that you have a fairy-tale heritage and a magical pumpkin carriage," he said quietly. "But I also know it might be a bit... overwhelming when you first find out about something like that. I'm guessing it feels rather confusing and weird inside your head right now. Just…try not to worry about it too much, okay? You don't need to have all the answers at once. You'll figure it out bit by bit. That's what I did. And if you ever want to talk about it to someone who understands, then, well, I'm pretty good at listening."

Bess felt a rush of warmth towards Louie. After all, he'd gone through something similar when he became a werewolf so he really could understand. And it was nice to hear someone say that it was okay to feel a little confused. It made it less scary somehow.

"Thanks." Bess smiled. "I'd like that."

Louie smiled back and they walked the last few steps to the mansion in silence. The black gates loomed up, tall and imposing. The iron bars were covered in signs telling people to keep out and turn back. Yet there was no sign of the Candymaker himself or anyone from the Train of Dark Wonders.

"I thought some of the others might be here by now," Bess said, looking around. "How do we know that Professor Ash hasn't already got the gobstopper? What if he's back at the train, waiting for us?"

"Dad would find some way of leaving us a message if that was the case," Louie said. "He'd probably use one of the bats…"

He trailed off and Bess followed his gaze to a familiar shape on the gate before them. Mish was hanging sound asleep, from one of the ornate curls of iron. The bumblebee bat had a little scroll of paper clutched in one tiny foot and was snoring contentedly.

"Well, well," Beau said. "Maybe we won't need to go inside. Perhaps the professor has beaten us to it."

He sounded more disappointed than relieved and Bess felt the same way. The black marble mansion sprawled before them looked quite scary, but it still seemed a shame to come so far and not get to see what was inside. Besides which, she still desperately needed to find something to feed her whispering flowers…

Louie stepped forward and gave Mish an affectionate rub on the head with his fingertip. The bat woke up and blinked sleepily for a moment, before giving a big yawn that showed off all his pointed teeth. He dropped the letter into Louie's hand, then spread his little wings to flutter up to the boy's shoulder. Louie unrolled the scroll and they all peered at it.

Dear children,

If you have journeyed to the Candymaker's mansion, then what were you thinking?

There are mere hours remaining until the door to this world closes. I would prefer that none of you were trapped here for the next hundred years, so please return to the train at once. It is waiting at the gate, ready to depart. I will retrieve the ghostly gobstopper and meet you there.

Yours affectionately,
Dad/Professor Ash

PS Please take Mish with you and make sure he doesn't do anything foolish.

Louie lowered the letter and looked up at the others. "I can't leave my dad here in a spooky mansion by himself," he said.

"You don't know that he's still in there," Maria pointed out. "He might already be back at the train, like Bess said."

Louie nodded. "He might. Or he could be in trouble inside that place. Besides, he doesn't know about the sugar bear the gummy queen told us about. If we don't find the sweet and destroy it, then the Candymaker might come up with some way of preventing us from leaving this land. I'm going in, but you can all head back of course."

The other three immediately protested that they wanted to stay and help.

"Don't be such a silly billy," Beau said, nudging Louie in the ribs. "How would you even get inside by yourself? I don't think your ghost violin will be much help in this situation."

"Well…my dad obviously thought he'd be able to get in somehow," Louie said, although he looked relieved at the thought of the others coming with him.

"We stick together," Maria insisted and Bess nodded vigorously.

They all turned their attention to the gates. They were far too high to climb and Bess was pleased to finally have the chance to use her lock-picking skills. But then, all of a sudden – impossibly – Beau was standing on the other side of the bars.

"Good news, everyone," he said, examining the gates. "It looks like I can open these from the inside."

There was a *thunk* as he slid back a bolt and then the gates creaked softly as he swung them open.

Bess stared. "How… How did you manage to—?"

"Climb over the gate? On account of my, er…my acrobat training. At theatre school."

Maria gave a cough that sounded very much like *ninja school*. And Bess thought Beau really must be a ninja after all. The gates were more than three metres high and he'd managed to flip himself over them without even making them rattle. She was impressed, but also disappointed not to have had a chance to be useful. Still, at least they were one step closer to getting inside. She wondered how Professor Ash had gained entry. Perhaps he'd found another way in or else had his own means of getting past locked gates.

The mansion gleamed shiny black in the sunlight. Bess looked up and thought she saw a shadowy shape flit past one of the top-floor windows. But Bess didn't feel an ounce of regret as the gates closed behind them with a clang. It didn't matter how spooky the mansion looked – they'd come this far and there was no turning back now.

Chapter 37

Asweeping drive led up to the mansion's front door, which the children followed, keeping a wary lookout as they went. They half expected the Candymaker himself to leap out at any moment and start committing nefarious deeds. The mansion had dozens of windows and he could be watching from any one of them.

"Maybe it'll be easy to get inside," Beau suggested in a quiet voice. "It seems like most of the creatures and ghosts around here stay out of his way. I don't think he'll be expecting intruders."

Bess was pretty sure it wasn't going to be as easy as all that, but they could always hope. They'd made it up to the front porch without anyone stopping them at least. A HAUNTED! DO NOT ENTER! sign hung on the door, which was flanked by a couple of stone dragons.

When Maria gripped the handle, they found it was locked.

Bess glanced at Beau. Unless he was able to ninja his way through the letterbox, he would be thwarted by the locked door just like the rest of them. But before Bess could even reach for her lock-picking kit, Beau had whipped his puppet mouse from his pocket and posted it nose first through the letterbox. They heard a muffled thump as it landed and then some squeaking and scuffling from within. The next moment, the mouse opened the door from the inside and it swung open on creaking hinges. Bess sighed. It looked like she might never get the chance to be useful.

"Great work," Louie said.

Mish had gone to sleep on his shoulder, so he scooped up the little bat and tucked him into his pocket for safekeeping. The ninja mouse somersaulted his way back into Beau's coat and then the four children crossed the threshold into the entrance hall.

Candles flickered in sconces fastened to the walls and red and black tiles gleamed on the floor. Bess realised the tiles must be made from boiled sweets as her shoes stuck to them slightly as they walked further inside. A huge sugar chandelier sparkled over their heads and a curved double staircase swept up to the floor above. The balustrades were made from barley twists and the smell of boiled sugar was strong in the air. There was still no sign of Professor Ash. Bess hoped that meant he'd already completed his mission and was now safely back on the train – not chained up in a dungeon somewhere.

"The almanac doesn't say anything about the mansion's layout," Beau whispered to the others. "I don't think anyone's ever been inside before."

"We should move quickly," Maria said. "We don't want to be in this place any longer than we have to. And the gate to our world will be closing soon."

They picked a direction at random and walked into the room on their right. It was a sitting room with a handsome collection of chocolate furniture set up round a cold fireplace. There was a grand-looking sofa and two large armchairs. The children were careful not to touch anything, but as they passed the furniture it all began to melt – and not slowly, but quickly. Big fat droplets ran down the sides and in a matter of minutes there were only puddles of chocolate on the floor where the furniture had been. The children stared in dismay.

"Well, that can't be good," Beau said. "Do you think it's some kind of alarm system?"

"If so, then it means Professor Ash must have come through the mansion a different way," Maria said. "Or else he'd have already triggered the alarm."

Bess suddenly had a very bad feeling. And yet...no one appeared to chase them away or gobble them up or turn them into sweets.

"Let's just keep moving," Louie said quietly.

They went on into the next room, which was really more of a chamber – Bess thought it must have been as big as the whole of the downstairs of her house. The walls were adorned with dragon wallpaper and in the middle of the floor was an amazing ship. It was an old-fashioned galleon, like the type a pirate might sail, and it was made entirely from chocolate. The hull, the mermaid figurehead, the anchor and masts were all carved from dark slabs, while the sails were fashioned from sheets of white chocolate.

Bess stared. "How could one person have made this? It must have taken hours and hours."

It was easily big enough for the children to climb aboard.

"Whatever you do, don't touch it," Beau warned. "We can't be too careful after the minty mummies and the pumpkin carriage. Absolutely no grabbing, touching, poking or licking."

They all kept their hands firmly clamped by their sides, but it didn't matter. As they tiptoed past the ship, it began to melt just as the chocolate furniture had done. Only there was a lot more chocolate this time and it created a wave that rushed towards their feet. They had to hurry into the next room in order to avoid being swept up in it. Maria slammed the door shut behind them and they all tried to ignore the little puddle of chocolate that began to seep underneath.

"The mansion is definitely reacting to us," Maria said. "You're right, Beau. It must be an alarm system. The Candymaker could be on his way – we need to get a move on."

They turned their attention to the new room. It was ordinary-sized and lined with shelves. These were full of jars containing an assortment of candy body parts. There were mostly ears with a few hands and feet thrown in too.

"This room is weird," Beau muttered. "But at least there's no chocolate to melt."

They rushed through the rest of the ground floor. In the kitchen, they found a family of sugar skeletons sitting round a table as if they were waiting for their dinner.

"Look, there's a sink," Bess pointed out. "If we find the sugar gummy bear, perhaps we can destroy it there."

But when Maria turned on the tap only hot fudge sauce came out. There were chocolate mice everywhere they looked too. Living ones that scuttled about, disappearing into holes in the skirting board with a flick of their long chocolate tails. Maybe they were all hurrying off to warn the Candymaker. But surely by now the magician knew they were here?

"This is odd," Bess said. "Where *is* the Candymaker? Why hasn't he come to stop us?"

"Maybe Dad has already…I don't know…tied him up and locked him in a cupboard or something," Louie suggested hopefully.

"Let's not worry about that for now," Maria said. "If he appears, then I'll set my fire lion on him."

In another room, the children found a selection of jelly snakes coiling down from the chandeliers, along with a sparkling collection of candy scarabs that Bess thought were quite beautiful. They were almost like jewels with their shimmering metallic-coloured shells. Bess wondered if the snakes or scarabs might make good food for her flowers, but she wasn't sure they were magical enough. They didn't seem to be doing much other than looking pretty.

"He really is a very talented candymaker," Maria said. "It's too bad he's evil."

"As least there's no sign of him yet," Beau said. "But then there's no sign of the gobstopper or the sugar gummy bear either."

"I think we've searched everywhere on the ground floor now," Louic said as they came back out into the entrance hall.

The double staircase loomed over them.

"Nothing for it," Beau said. "We're going to have to go upstairs."

Chapter 38

The children crept up to the first floor as quietly as they could. Bess couldn't help thinking about the spooky secrets and strange sights that might be tucked away upstairs. She had visions of attics full of haunted dolls, ghostly women wearing wedding dresses and headless horsemen – any one of which would be pretty cool to see up close but bound to get in the way when it came to finding the sugar gummy bear and the ghostly gobstopper.

But here, at last, they found the Candymaker's personal collections. There was room after room of fantastical sweets, all tucked away inside glass domes, each one clearly labelled in neat handwriting. The children walked past a lunatic lollipop, a horrifying humbug, a petrifying pear drop and a murderous mint that snarled at them and threw itself against the glass in a ferocious manner. Bess's fingers itched to take something for her whispering flowers back at the museum, but she didn't want to do anything that might trigger an alarm prematurely. Hopefully, she'd be able to grab something on the way out.

Finally, they found a label for the ghostly gobstopper, but to their dismay, it lay on the ground among the smashed glass of its dome.

"It's all right," Louie said. "It must have been Dad. The Candymaker wouldn't need to break into his own display case, would he?"

When they got closer to it, they saw that another note had been left for them.

Dear children,

If you are reading this note, then I am very disappointed, but not at all surprised, that you ignored my first instruction to go back to the train.

This time though you really must listen. I have the ghostly gobstopper and am returning to the train directly. I expect to see you all there within the hour. I shall be really very cross if you end up stranded in this land.

Yours affectionately,
Dad/Professor Ash

PS Go now. Absolutely no delays, heroics or
last-minute adventures.

"Well, that's that then," Beau said. "We've got what we came to this land for. We should do what the professor says and get back to the train."

"Professor Ash might have taken the ghostly gobstopper, but he doesn't have the sugar bear," Bess pointed out.

Given what the gummy queen had told them, she still didn't like the idea of leaving without first destroying the sweet. She gazed round the room and then, with an exclamation of triumph, pointed at a glass dome beside the window. "There it is!"

And there indeed sat a gigantic sparkling sweet the size of a melon. It was shaped like a gummy bear, but made entirely from sugar. The children hurried over to look. Just like the gummy queen had said, it had a little red heart tucked in the middle of its chest. But, before they could examine it properly, Cedric flew down to the window sill and blew out an excited little stream of fire.

The children saw that he'd spotted Flossie. The old dragon hadn't flown to the mountains like the gummy queen had told them she would. Instead, she was down in the mansion's garden, sprawled on her side on the grass, while a man stood over her in a threatening manner.

It could only be the Candymaker. Bess could see his candy hand, which was larger than the other one and bright pink in colour, made from the same gummy sweets they'd seen elsewhere throughout this world. He wore sunglasses to protect his sugar eyes and was dressed in a midnight black suit with an orange tie. Tiny pumpkins adorned the rim of his dark top hat and he was surrounded by a little cloud of puffed-up marshmallow ghosts. Bess guessed that he must be using his candy magic on Flossie because the dragon wasn't even trying to defend herself. She just lay there, panting, waiting for the Candymaker to do his worst.

"Why did she come here?" Bess groaned. "She was free!"

"We've got to destroy the sugar bear now!" Beau gasped. "If he loses his powers, then he won't be able to hurt Flossie."

He broke the glass dome with his elbow and snatched up the bear.

"We'll take it to one of the fountains," Beau went on. "That's the only place where I've seen water. At least it *looked* like water when the Easter eagles flew us over."

Before they could take a single step, there was a growling sound behind them. It seemed that they had finally been discovered. As they all turned slowly towards the doorway, Bess had visions of some sort of guard dog, but it was much worse than that. The Candymaker had a guard *bear*. A big black bear made from liquorice.

The beast lumbered a few steps closer to them, still growling. At once, Maria conjured her fire lion. He appeared in a burning blast of orange flame and roared so fiercely that even the murderous mint trembled in its glass dome. In response, the bear rose up on its hind legs and let out a bellow of its own.

"Come on!" Beau yanked open the window.

"We're on the first floor!" Maria gasped. "And we're not ninjas so how are we supposed to—"

But Beau had already grabbed a puppet from his coat pocket and set him on the window sill. Bess recognised the magician she'd seen back in Roseville. Only he wasn't conjuring paper roses this time, but a paper staircase. The steps rapidly unfolded one after the other, like a Slinky, until they reached all the way down to the ground.

"Will it hold our weight?" Bess asked dubiously.

"Trust me!" Beau said. "Paper is really strong if it's folded up into the right shape. And my magician knows what he's doing."

Bess cast one last longing look back at the sweets. Any one of them would have made excellent food for her whispering flowers, but there was no way to snatch one without going past the bear. So she followed the others as they tumbled out of the window and on to the staircase. The bear let out another bellow behind them, but the fire lion blocked its path, roaring fiercely. Thankfully, Beau had been right about the staircase being strong enough – even if it did sway alarmingly underfoot – and soon the children had reached the lawn. Unfortunately, though, all the commotion had drawn the Candymaker's attention to them.

He turned round and Bess flinched in fear. The sun flashed upon his sunglasses, but she could tell he was unhappy to see them from the way his mouth turned down at the edges. Then he spotted the sugar bear tucked under Beau's arm and he didn't just frown, he yelled.

"Hey! Put down that bear!"

But Beau was off, running as fast as he could towards a fountain. The Candymaker abandoned Flossie to chase after him. Bess hoped the dragon would take the opportunity to fly away, but she just stayed sprawled on the grass. Perhaps the Candymaker had already hurt her somehow.

Beau shot to the fountain as fast as a hare, but the Candymaker was hot on his heels.

"Don't!" he hollered, making a dive for Beau.

The Candymaker grabbed the back of Beau's coat, dragging him to the ground, but as he fell Beau hurled the sugar bear into the fountain. It landed with a satisfying splash. The children all held their breath, desperately hoping that it was indeed water in the fountain and not some other kind of liquid… But, to their immense relief, the sugar bear began to dissolve, quickly breaking up into lumps until only the red heart remained. Before long, that had melted away to nothing too.

Bess felt a cheer rise in her throat. They'd done it! And without his sugar powers perhaps they stood a chance of escaping the Candymaker and getting back to the train before the gate closed.

But something was wrong. The Candymaker didn't seem angry so much as distraught. His sunglasses had fallen off when he'd tackled Beau to the ground, and he raised his gummy hand to his face to shield his sugar eyes.

"What have you done?" he gasped.

Flossie finally heaved herself to her feet, but instead of flying to freedom, she shuffled over to where the Candymaker's sunglasses had fallen in the grass. Bess watched as she carefully picked them up in one pink jelly claw and then held them out to the Candymaker. He took them gratefully and pressed them back on to his face.

"Thanks, old girl," he said, reaching out to give her snout a rub with his knuckles.

Bess glanced at the others. Something was definitely wrong here. Why was he being nice to the dragon? And why had Flossie come here in the first place? Bess could tell from the uncertain expressions on their faces that they were wondering the same thing.

"How did you children even get here?" the Candymaker asked. "The gate to other worlds isn't due to open for another week."

"It opened almost three days ago," Louie said.

"Did it?" The Candymaker sounded incredulous. Then he slapped his candy hand to his forehead and groaned. "I must have made a mistake in my calculations. But that still doesn't explain why you would destroy the sugar bear. Do you *want* to have your ears stolen away?"

Bess thought of the jars of candy ears they'd seen back in the mansion and shuddered.

"Er, no," Maria said. "We like our ears right where they are, thanks very much."

"But… But I don't understand!" the Candymaker said. "Why would you break my enchantment over the ghostly gummy bears?"

"Because what you did to them wasn't right," Beau said.

"What *I* did?" the Candymaker exclaimed. Flossie had flumped down by his feet and was making the purring sound they'd heard before.

"We know that your Halloween sweets destroyed the gummy bears' land," Maria said. "And that you double-crossed them at the queen's Jubilee Picnic. We heard it all from the queen herself."

The Candymaker shook his head. "You've got it all wrong," he said. "The bears were ghosts before I arrived. And yes, I double-crossed them at the Jubilee Picnic, but only because they were hunting children."

"Hunting children?" Bess frowned. "But why would they do that?"

"Because they wanted revenge," the Candymaker replied simply. "On the children who eat gummy bears. Especially those who take great delight in biting off the different body parts one by one. If you give a ghostly gummy bear half a chance, it will steal away the ears of any child it comes into contact with. They were using the Troll Network to go after children in other worlds before I came along.

"The queen asked me to provide an ear-themed spread – ear cupcakes, ear muffins, sugar ears, chocolate ears and so on. I only pretended to go along with it so I could place a spell on the bears. An enchantment so that they would never hurt any other children again. It took months and months of preparation." He stared at the last sad lumps of sugar dissolving in the fountain. "And now you've undone it all. Whatever the gummy queen told you, it was a lie. She tricked you."

Beau shook his head. "But... But if you're not evil, then why do you have a haunted mansion with a ferocious guard bear prowling the corridors?"

The Candymaker blinked. "I like haunted mansions. And he isn't a guard bear. He's just a bear. His name is Ollie and he wouldn't hurt a candy worm."

Bess glanced back at the mansion and saw the bear peering out of the window at them. There was no sign of the fire lion and she guessed that Maria had ended the spell.

"He growled at us," Beau said.

"Well, he does that when he wants to play. Which is most of the time. A bit like Flossie here. Although these days she spends more time snoozing, I imagine."

The old dragon had indeed closed her eyes and was sound asleep, looking perfectly content in the sun. Bess thought of how Flossie had headed straight for the mansion and how affectionate she'd been to the Candymaker.

"Before we let her out of the caves, the gummy queen told us that Flossie was her pet," Bess said. "That's not true either, is it? She belongs to you."

The Candymaker nodded. "After the Jubilee Picnic, Queen Pittipat sent me a letter to say that Flossie had been killed and I believed her. I'm so very glad to see her again. I've had many candy dragons, but Flossie is my most beloved. Queen Pittipat must have let her go, knowing that she'd come here and I would be distracted by her arrival, thus giving you a chance to break in. I'd have noticed you going into the mansion otherwise and stopped you before you could get to the sugar bear."

Bess guessed he must have already been busy with Flossie when Professor Ash passed through the mansion.

"Can you make another?" Louie asked, looking worried. "Are you in danger from the gummy bears yourself?"

"Oh, I'll be fine," the Candymaker replied. "I have my marshmallow ghosts to protect me. But it will take time to make another sugar bear and by then it will be too late."

"What do you mean too late?" Bess asked.

The Candymaker gave her a serious look. "My dear girl, isn't it obvious? The gummy bears don't want to stay here with me. They want to escape to a world with lots of unsuspecting children to steal ears from." He pointed at the sky. "Even as we speak, they're heading towards the gateway to your world. And now that my enchantment is broken, there's nothing I can do to stop them."

Bess and the others looked up and saw that the Candymaker was right. All around, gummy-bear ghosts were rising up into the air like strange little hot-air balloons – and they were flying straight in the direction of the gateway and the Train of Dark Wonders.

ChaPTeR 39

"**T**his is bad!" Beau groaned. "There's hours left until sunset. Hundreds of those bears might pass through the gate before it closes."

"Actually, that's not quite accurate," the Candymaker said. "It's Moonday today. That means the sun sets early. There isn't long to go at all. There's perhaps twenty minutes of daylight left."

Bess felt a rising sense of panic. It was good that the gummy ghosts would have less time to get through the gate, but it also meant that they were in danger of getting left behind too.

"I can stop the gummy bears!" Louie said. "In fact, I can get rid of them for good – but I'll need my black violin."

"To the train then," Beau said. "What are we waiting for?"

"You'll never make it in time," the Candymaker said sadly. "Perhaps Flossie can take you – if she's not too tired. I'll see if I can wake her—"

"We don't need Flossie!" Bess said, frantically rummaging in her backpack. "We have a carriage."

She grabbed hold of the little black silk bag and slipped out the pumpkin. Just as the fairy godmother had said, the instant her hands touched it, the pumpkin transformed into the gleaming carriage they had seen before.

"Great idea!" Maria exclaimed. "I'll create the horses."

Cedric perched on her shoulder, his little snout sniffing the air as Maria raised her hands and prepared for more fire magic. Sparks flew between her fingers as she muttered a string of magic words and the next moment a pair of magnificent fire horses reared up before their eyes. Their manes and tails were orange streams of flame, and they looked wild, fierce and fast. The carriage's harness uncurled to attach itself to the horses' bridles. The Candymaker hurried ahead to open the gates and the children raced to the carriage, tumbling into the purple velvet interior.

They took their seats and Bess found herself pressed up against a small side table beneath one of the windows, set with a dainty china dish piled high with sugared plums. A raven perched beside this, sleek and glossy, with feathers so black that they had a bluish tint. He looked right at Bess with bright, intelligent eyes.

"About time, Elizabeth Harper," he said in a croaky voice. "I'm Jet."

Bess had never seen a talking raven before and normally would have been delighted by something so unusual, even if it was using her full name, but there wasn't time for chitchat now. "Hello," she gasped. "I can't wait to get to know you, but we're in somewhat of a hurry—"

"Huh." The raven seemed unsurprised. "Wicked stepsisters usually are. Say no more, mistress – we'll talk later."

"To the train!" Maria shouted and the horses took off at once.

"Good luck," the Candymaker called as they passed through the gates, giving an encouraging wave with his candy hand.

The carriage hurtled down the road away from the mansion at a dizzying speed. Bess saw the churches and graveyards pass by in a blur of colours. And there wasn't a moment to lose. When she peered up into the sky, she saw dozens of the ghostly gummy bears flying above them towards the train. Luckily gummy bears weren't as fast as fire horses. The carriage overtook them, but the bears were so focused on the gateway that they didn't seem to notice it passing beneath them. Or perhaps they didn't think it mattered.

Now that the sugar bear was gone, the gummy ghosts probably thought they had a clear escape route into another world. Bess shuddered at the thought of what she and her friends might have accidentally unleashed and the havoc it would cause back home. The image of little kids cowering in their beds, terrified of having their ears stolen away, all because of what they'd done, was terrible. They had to get back in time to fix their mistake.

Maria's fire horses flew across the land at a tremendous gallop and soon enough the Train of Dark Wonders came into view, waiting at the gateway.

Bess's carriage skidded to a stop alongside the train and the four children clambered out. Bess said the words to transform it back into a pumpkin, taking the raven with it, while Maria dismissed the fire horses. At their arrival, Professor Ash poked his head out of the locomotive window. He looked a little frazzled as he called out to them.

"I do wish you'd occasionally take notice of my instructions. Hurry up and climb aboard. These gummy bears don't look friendly."

"They're not!" Louie called back. "We've got a plan, but you need to get the train ready to go – the sun sets early today. There's probably only minutes to go!"

Bess was relieved that Professor Ash didn't waste time asking questions, but immediately disappeared back into the locomotive. Seconds later, the train whistle gave one long blast instructing people to return to the carriages and the funnel began to billow steam.

The children raced towards the boys' sleeping compartment, where Louie's black violin was kept. Some of the train's crew called out greetings and questions from the windows as they ran by, but there was no time to reply. When they reached the carriage, Beau somersaulted in through the window and threw Louie's violin out to him.

And not a second too soon. The gummy-bear ghosts had caught up and were diving down towards the gateway, with Queen Pittipat in the lead. Her fur-lined cape flew out behind her and the jewels in her necklace and sandals glittered dangerously. She looked fierce and cruel and Bess wondered how they ever could have trusted her.

In one fluid movement, Louie tucked the violin beneath his chin, lifted the bow and started to play. It was strange, chilling music that made Bess shiver all over. And it had the most extraordinary effect on the bears. They all clapped their paws over their ears and howled as if the music were painful to them.

And then, one by one, they began to pop like big gummy balloons. One moment the bears were there and the next they had vanished completely, leaving only a faint candy scent.

Finally, only Queen Pittipat remained. She seemed to be stronger than the other bears and she was absolutely furious about what Louie had done.

Bess glanced around in a panic, looking for something to stop her. But what could she use against a ghost? Maria conjured up a flock of firebirds, but these passed straight through the gummy queen with no effect at all. The arrows from Beau's archer puppet were just as useless.

"How *dare* you?" she snarled. "You'll pay for this, you mangy wolf."

And then she dived through the air towards Louie with a horrid, piercing screech so loud and furious that it shattered the train's windows. People jumped back as glass flew in all directions.

Louie stared up at the queen with an expression of dread, but he kept playing the music faster and faster. Bess wasn't sure what the queen was going to do exactly, but she clearly intended to hurt him. Perhaps she was going to steal away one of his ears like the Candymaker had said.

Bess's eyes suddenly fell on the train's broken windows and they reminded her of the haunted doll's house back at the Odditorium. And the thought of the house made her think of the ghost pepper.

Her hand flew to the tiny bottle dangling from her necklace. There was no time to wonder whether it would work or whether this was a good idea. Bess tugged hard to snap the necklace's clasp and yanked the tiny cork from the bottle.

She leaped in front of Louie with only seconds to spare. The gummy queen was still howling and Bess caught a horrible glimpse inside her mouth. It was full of rows of razor-sharp teeth.

"Interfering little brats!" the queen screeched. "How would you like it if someone came along and bit off your legs or your head...or your ears?"

Bess yelled as the gummy bear clamped her teeth down on her ear.

Wincing in pain, Bess threw the contents of the bottle at Queen Pittipat. Both Bess and Louie immediately started sneezing violently. Louie's bow scraped over his violin strings as he struggled to continue playing. Queen Pittipat jerked back, releasing Bess's ear. It throbbed and stung, but was thankfully still attached to her head.

For a horrible moment, Bess thought that it wasn't going to work. Maybe the ghost pepper would have no effect on a gummy-bear ghost? Queen Pittipat gave a snarl, baring her sharp, pointy teeth, and Bess felt ridiculous for thinking that she could be useful in a situation as strange and desperate as this…

But then, all of a sudden, the queen let out a gigantic sneeze. "You, girl, wh-what was—?" she spluttered. "What was in that b—? *ACHOOOOO!*"

She let out a roar of a sneeze so big and ferocious that it caused her to pop, just like the other bears. One moment she was there – the next she'd vanished in a puff of purple fluffy smoke.

ChaPTeR 40

There was no chance to celebrate. The train gave another urgent blast on its whistle. Time had run out and the gate would close at any moment. Bess could see the sun already starting its rapid descent.

"Quick!" Louie gasped, grabbing Bess's hand. "On to the train!"

Maria hurried to join them and the three children gripped the window sill of the sleeper carriage to drag themselves up through the window of the boys' compartment. Beau reached over to help pull them inside and they landed in a tangled heap on the floor. They scrambled to their feet and stared out of the window. The train seemed to be going painfully slowly and Bess felt a sickening lurch in her stomach as the sky darkened. What if they didn't quite make it in time and were doomed to spend the rest of their lives in the Land of Halloween Sweets? Her parents would be devastated.

But then the train jerked forward and it quickly picked up speed until it was whizzing through the gate and into the corkscrew tunnel beyond. The final carriage made it through just as the gate clanged closed behind them and the children all breathed out a sigh of relief. Nobody was in a hurry to visit that land again any time soon.

"Your ear!" Louie cried, looking at Bess. "It's bleeding!"

"I think it'll be all right with some of the professor's special ointment," Maria said, leaning closer to assess the damage. "The queen's teeth didn't bite through the ear. I bet it stings like mad though. Are you okay? That was very brave."

"I'm okay," Bess replied. "I'm just glad it worked. I've never used ghost pepper on an actual ghost before."

"Thank you," Louie said. He gave her shoulder a squeeze. "Maria's right – that was really brave. I thought I was going to lose an ear for sure when she flew at me like that." He shuddered. "Who would have thought that gummy bears could be so nasty?"

"Well done, Bess," Beau added. "That was quite something. You moved so fast back there that people are probably going to start thinking you're a ninja too."

"I hope Mish didn't get too squashed in all the commotion," Louie said. He rummaged in his pocket and drew out the little bat, who was still curled up in a happy, sleepy ball.

"Speaking of bats," Beau said, "we should go and find your dad. I imagine we'll have some explaining and apologising to do. But I'm sure he'll understand when we tell him about the evil gummy bears and saving Flossie."

Bess followed the others out into the corridor. Through the windows she could see the gigantic roots of the redwood trees winding down through the tunnel. She remembered what Beau had told her about them being in California and her heart sank at the thought of how soon they'd be back in England. The adventure was over. Life would continue on the train as normal for the others, but Bess would have to go home.

She was feeling quite glum by the time they entered Professor Ash's office. But his special ointment took the sting out of her ear and Beau did a good job of explaining things so that they didn't get told off – at least not too much.

It helped that Professor Ash was in a very good mood because of the ghostly gobstopper. The children all crowded round excitedly to take a look at it. It was the same size as the ones Bess had seen back in Roseville's sweetshop, only this one wasn't white and speckled with colours. It was a bright, shining silver – just like the full moon. There were even little craters in it.

"We did it, my boy," Professor Ash said, clapping Louie on the shoulder. "With any luck, you'll never have to be locked up in the red carriage again. Although I must say I feel rather bad about stealing it from the Candymaker now that I know he wasn't evil after all. But hopefully he'd agree that the freedom of his pet dragon is a suitable trade. I did think it was surprisingly easy to take the gobstopper."

"You're lucky you didn't come across that gigantic liquorice bear," Beau said.

"Oh, but I did," the professor said. "I befriended him in fact. Threw his ball down the corridor a couple of times. I suppose you all panicked and believed him to be dangerous?"

The children shuffled their feet sheepishly, then Beau deliberately changed the subject by saying, "What does the gobstopper taste like? It smells like moon dust."

Louie picked it up from his dad's desk and licked it. And that was the moment they all realised the sweet did something they hadn't known about. Not only would it allow Louie to stay in control when he turned into a werewolf, but it also allowed him to transform into a wolf whenever he liked even if it wasn't a full moon. One moment it was Louie standing there – and the next it was the wolf.

Except Louie was in control this time. There was no snarling or growling at all, only snuffling and lots of tail wagging. He bounded about the carriage excitedly and then shot straight out of the door, eager to explore the train in his wolf form for the first time. Laughing, Maria and Beau hurried after him. Bess would have liked to have gone too, but she had more important things on her mind.

"Professor Ash?" she began. "I know we agreed I could only go on one adventure with the train before returning home, but I didn't manage to collect any magical food in the Land of Halloween Sweets. And my poisoned-apple tree still doesn't have any fruit. I've got nothing to give my whispering flowers. The Odditorium will be torn down in under a month unless I can find something to feed them."

Professor Ash waved Bess over to one of the armchairs and sat down opposite her. "From what you've told me, it sounds like you passed by many magical sweets – the raining frogs, Frankenmints and so on. Don't you have a minty mummy asleep in your bag at this very moment?"

"Yes, but I can't possibly feed him to the flowers. He's alive and so were the frogs. It would be too cruel."

"Well, I certainly applaud your ethics," said Professor Ash. "The minty mummy is a marvellous specimen and it would be a very great shame if the little fellow were to be fed to flowers. I can absolutely help you to procure some magic beans. They're very common and can be found in almost all the lands we've visited so far. It's difficult for us to leave straight away though. There's maintenance to be done on the train and some of the staff are due to return home to visit their families.

"It's a pity you didn't pick up any of the candy beetles," the professor went on. "You must have seen them? They seemed to be growing on pretty much every bush in the Land of Halloween Sweets. They appear ordinary enough, but actually they have plenty of magic. If you drop them into water, they turn into candy octopuses. And if you throw them up in the air they turn into birds and so on. They're a shape-shifting candy. I only found out by accident when one of them fell in my tea. They don't seem to be sentient though."

"Oh, but I *do* have some candy beetles!" Bess exclaimed. "We filled our bags with them for dinner."

She rummaged in her backpack and moved the green pumpkin out of the way to get to the beetle sweets. They made quite a large pile when she took them all out. She was sure the others would let her have the beetles they'd collected too. Professor Ash selected one and dropped it into a glass of water on his desk and it immediately turned into a fish, then a stingray, before finally settling on an octopus.

"Well, they should keep your flowers going for a while," Professor Ash said. "And I'm sure we can pick up some magic beans for you when we travel to the next land. I'll drop them off at the station under the Odditorium."

Bess was about to ask whether there was any chance she might be allowed to travel with the train again when Professor Ash said, "That was a particularly splendid carriage you arrived in. How did you come by it?"

When Bess told him about the godmother for the fairy-tale villains, he seemed unsurprised. Nor was he shocked when Bess told him about her own heritage.

"You already knew, didn't you?" she said.

"I did," Professor Ash replied. "Your grandfather shared the same bloodline. He confided in me when he joined the train."

"Where exactly did Pops join the train?" Bess asked. "Was it from our world or…or a different one?"

After all, evil queens and wicked stepsisters didn't actually exist – they were just storybook people. Come to think of it, magic beans were from a different place altogether too.

Professor Ash gave her a thoughtful look. "You're a smart girl, Bess," he finally said. "I think you're already on your way to figuring out the answer. Yes, your grandfather came from a different world to the one you grew up in. I first met him when the Train of Dark Wonders was searching for Echo – the carousel horse you rode. I gather your pops never told you any of this himself?"

Bess shook her head. "No." She thought of the fairy-tale map she'd seen briefly before he bundled it away in his desk. "Pops never said a word. I'm not sure whether my dad and uncle even know."

"Perhaps that was a part of his life he wanted to leave behind," Professor Ash said. "Maybe it's better that way. Only…"

"Only what?" Bess asked, eager for any titbits of information.

"I hesitate to say anything I oughtn't," Professor Ash said with a slight frown, "but I remember Henry telling me about the whispering flowers from the Land of Fairy Tales. They're not merely an interesting oddity. In their world, they're used mostly as…well, as a sort of security system. For something in need of guarding. I just wondered whether your grandfather ever mentioned there being anything in particular at the Odditorium that needed this protection?"

The professor was watching her closely. Bess thought back over everything her pops had said about the whispering flowers, but couldn't remember him ever telling her that they were guarding anything.

"In his letter, he said they were the most important exhibit at the Odditorium," she said. "But I thought he was talking about what might happen if they ran out of food."

"Hmm. Well, perhaps that's it," Professor Ash said, although he still looked faintly troubled. "Best keep an eye out though. There are many secret rooms and hidden chambers in the Odditorium. Not to mention the disguised staircases and concealed corridors and so on."

Bess waved a hand. "I know where all those are."

"Do you?" Professor Ash replied. "Might there not be certain parts your pops never showed you?"

Bess paused. She'd always assumed she knew the Odditorium inside out. It was a disconcerting thought that there might be little pockets of it she was unaware of, but the more she thought about it, the more it seemed possible. She hadn't known about the station after all.

"The chances are Henry collected the whispering flowers purely because he thought they'd make an interesting curiosity," Professor Ash said briskly. "Now I won't keep you from your friends any longer. We'll arrive at Roseville soon and I'm sure you wish to spend the remaining time with them."

Bess was disappointed that he wasn't going to tell her anything else about where Pops had come from, but she was also itching to get back to the others. As she said goodbye to the professor, she wondered whether this was why she'd always felt so out of place in Roseville. Maybe it wasn't where she really belonged at all... But for now she swallowed down her questions and went off in search of her friends.

"Being able to turn into a wolf whenever you like is definitely going to come in handy," Beau said.

The four children were gathered round one of the rooftop fires as the train chugged along through a troll tunnel.

"I'm not using my wolf side to scare people, if that's what you're thinking," Louie said mildly.

"Well, not usually," Beau agreed. "But just think about it. Next time we're in an enchanted land and you come face to face with a gruesome hedgehog or a rampaging Frankenmint who won't be reasoned with, it might be quite handy to turn yourself into a snarling wolf before their eyes."

"Even so," Louie replied, "I won't deliberately scare people. The whole point of the ghostly gobstopper was to avoid that."

Beau rolled his eyes. "Being a werewolf is wasted on you," he grumbled.

"Well, being a ninja is wasted on you," Maria pointed out. "I think I'm the only one who really uses my full talents properly. And Bess of course."

"Are you all right?" Louie asked, looking at Bess. "You seem a bit down even though we banished the gummy bears and got the gobstopper. And you found food for your flowers in the end, didn't you?"

Bess was sitting with a blanket wrapped round her shoulders and Spooky purring in a contented ball on her lap. The ghost cat had barely left her side all evening.

"I'm really pleased the mission was a success," Bess said. "I'm just sad it's over. I'm going to miss all of you and the train and everything. It'll be hard going back to normal after this."

The others fell silent and a gloomy air settled on them.

"It's not fair," Maria finally said. "You should be allowed to stay on the train."

"I have to go back," Bess said. "I'm glad that I have something to feed my flowers, but I'm not sure whether it will be enough to save the Odditorium. Nobody was visiting before – they seemed bored with all the exhibits. I suppose I do have the minty mummy. That'll be something new."

Louie shook his head. "You've got a lot more than just the minty mummy."

"What do you mean?"

Louie glanced at the others.

"We've been talking about it," Maria said. "And we've come up with some ideas for new exhibits. I'm going to make you a fire whale."

"Oh! Are you serious?" Bess gasped, delighted. "Thank you!"

Maria grinned. "It'll be a fire fish to begin with," she said. "Easier to transport that way. But once it's been in the Odditorium an hour or two it should transform into a whale."

"And I got you one of my werewolf fangs," Louie said, holding out his hand to reveal a massive, shining tooth.

Bess took the fang. "This is amazing. But it must have hurt pulling this out and don't you need all your teeth?"

"It's okay." Louie grinned. "They grow back."

"And I'd like to give you one of my puppets," Beau said.

"Really?" Bess said, thinking of the puppet magician and how it had drawn a crowd in the rose garden.

"Why not?" Beau replied. "You helped us. It's only fair that we return the favour. I thought you could have André, my puppet chef. He only has one speciality and it's soup so he wouldn't be any use for your flowers. But you mentioned that you'd like the Odditorium to have a café and André's pirate soup might be a good place to start."

"Pirate soup?" Bess exclaimed.

"It's quite delicious," Maria said. "It tastes like chicken soup mostly, but the really cool thing about André's pirate soup is that it comes with a little pirate galleon floating on top."

"There's even a tiny pirate crew on board," Louie said.

"You've just got to keep an eye on them because they're quite prone to firing the cannons whenever they feel like it," Beau put in. "Each cannon is about the size of a raisin." He held up his thumb and finger to demonstrate. "So you don't need to worry about it actually hurting anyone, but it might sting a little bit and leave a mosquito-bite-sized mark."

"Sometimes there's a mini mermaid swimming about in the soup too," Maria added. "And if she starts singing then you'll have to watch out that your customers don't try to drown themselves in the soup. It can be quite a tricky meal to eat actually, what with all the little cannonballs flying about and the enchanted mermaid singing. It's quite a spectacle though."

"It sounds incredible." Bess suddenly had a bit of a lump in her throat. A lovely warm feeling swept over her at the effort her friends were prepared to make for her. "Thank you so much," she said.

For the first time in a long while, Bess felt as if she'd found a place where she belonged. It had been a wonderful adventure, but she knew she couldn't stay. It was time to go home.

ChapTer 41

Bess walked through the corridors of Harper's Odditorium, humming one of the spooky tunes from Louie's ghost violin to herself. Two weeks had passed since she'd returned home. It was the Odditorium's grand reopening tomorrow and she wanted to make sure everything was ready. The last of the leaves and twigs had been cleared from the corridors and the whispering flowers had been very happy with the candy beetles. Together with Jamie, she had spent an entire afternoon walking around feeding them. Sure enough, the flowers had retreated through the windows with something of a sheepish air and gone back to climbing the walls of the building, softly whispering their endless supply of secrets.

"How was it then?" Jamie had asked while they fed the flowers. "The train? Everything you'd hoped?"

"It was wonderful," Bess replied. "But I think you already knew that. Have you travelled on it too?"

Jamie took a candy beetle from the bag and tossed it to the nearest flower. "Not much point denying it, I suppose."

"Did you come from the same place as Pops?"

Jamie nodded slowly. "That I did, miss."

"Please tell me what it was like," Bess begged.

But Jamie shook his head. "There's a reason your pops didn't like to talk about it. The Land of Fairy Tales…it's not what you imagine it would be from the books." A haunted expression swept over his face and he spoke the next words in almost a whisper. "It's a fearsome place. Best left well alone."

Try as she might, Bess couldn't persuade him to say more on the subject. It was incredibly frustrating. Pops had told her so many wonderful stories, but the most fascinating one of all he'd kept secret and she couldn't understand why. She would have loved to hear more about the world her family originally came from, but even the raven from the fairy godmother was no help.

"Ember created me just for you, mistress," Jet told her.

Bess had opened up the carriage again as soon as the flowers were dealt with and put it on display in one of the exhibition rooms.

"My life began in the Land of Halloween Sweets," the raven said. "I don't know much more about the fairy-tale world than you do. All I know is that I'm destined to be your loyal companion and serve you in any way I can. As long as you don't shrink the carriage into a pumpkin with me inside it again." The raven gave a huffy sniff. "That was rude."

"Oh, I'm sorry," Bess replied. "I'm very glad to have you for my companion of course and please call me Bess. I was really hoping to find out a bit more about my family history. What about the book that Ember mentioned? Do you know where it is?"

Apart from the sugared plums, Bess hadn't seen anything inside the carriage, but Jet immediately pointed with his beak to a hidden compartment under the seats where a large volume was stored. Bess pulled it out and gazed at the purple velvet cover. The title was stamped in black letters: *The Comprehensive Guide to Being a Wicked Stepsister (and Changing the World)*.

Bess's hands tightened round the book and she felt a great swell of excitement rising in her chest. When she flicked to the contents page, she saw that the chapter headings covered a fascinating range of things, from "The Care and Keeping of Talking Ravens" to "Poisoned Apples and Their Uses". She couldn't wait to dive in, but she had other matters to attend to regarding the Odditorium first.

Since she was no longer in breach of any safety regulations, the council had had no choice but to withdraw their threat of demolition. To Bess's immense satisfaction, Uncle Norman had been furious. But, even after the flowers had been sorted out, Bess had decided to keep the museum closed for another couple of weeks so that she could move some things around to make room for the new café. As promised, Beau had given her André, his puppet chef, and the pirate soup was everything she'd hoped it would be. She couldn't wait for the visitors to try it. Not only that, but she was looking forward to seeing their reaction to her new exhibits – the stepsister's carriage as well as the minty mummy, Louie's fang and Maria's spectacular fire whale.

Bess had taken down the whale skeleton hanging in the lobby and now the fire whale drifted lazily to and fro up near the ceiling, singing happily to herself. If all that wasn't enough to draw people into the Odditorium, then Bess didn't know what was. She was quietly confident. These exhibits were nothing like the ones the museum had housed before. They weren't dusty relics and they weren't locked behind glass. They were living, breathing wonders that visitors could get right up close to and even touch. No one had ever seen anything like them before and Bess was certain that people would come from miles around.

She walked through the museum to make sure that everything was in order. Jet perched on her shoulder, offering unsolicited advice and various nit-picking criticisms (something he was prone to).

"You know, I'm sure people would love to see you too," she told him. "I don't think anyone in Roseville will have met a talking raven before."

Unfortunately Jet got in a bit of a huff about this, taking offence at the notion that he might be an exhibit.

"I only meant that you're very handsome and fascinating," Bess said.

But Jet wouldn't be placated and took himself off to perch on top of Jessie's case. The raven and the haunted doll had taken quite a shine to one another so Bess left them to it, collected her flyers and went out of the front doors. Jet could get in and out through the Odditorium's many chimneys so she locked them behind her, knowing that he'd come and find her when he stopped sulking.

He was quite a sulky bird in general, but Bess didn't mind his moods and thought he was absolutely marvellous. Her parents had accepted him with resignation and her dad had even built a little perch for him in Bess's bedroom. Bess enjoyed the raven's company and it helped to have something magical to talk to when she was missing the train and her friends there.

Everything had been so interesting and exciting during her travels with them that a small part of her had hoped Roseville might somehow be different too when she got back, but it was exactly the same as it had always been. Her mum and dad had been very pleased to see her and no one at school had even noticed that she'd been gone, thanks to the scarecrow.

Her parents were expecting her home in time for lunch, but there was still an hour to go before that so Bess had just enough time to hand out the flyers round the rose garden. She'd designed them herself and was rather proud of them. She'd made sure not to give too much away, but she'd promised new and exciting exhibits at the Odditorium's reopening.

It was a sunny day and the rose garden was busy as expected. Bess got to work handing out the flyers and tried not to mind about the lukewarm reception to them. But it was impossible not to feel disappointed – and indignant – when she realised that some people were putting them straight into the nearest bin. How was she ever going to impress anyone with her new additions if she couldn't even get people through the front doors? She frowned up at the rose bushes, remembering Beau's puppet magician. Perhaps she would need to put on some sort of display herself. Maybe she could set the minty mummy free to stagger about, grumbling and groaning, near the duck pond?

She was so engrossed in her thoughts that she didn't notice Horace sitting on a nearby bench until he stuck out his foot and tripped her up. Bess went sprawling and her remaining flyers fluttered everywhere, tossed in all directions by the breeze. Several of them landed in the pond.

"*Grand Reopening*." Horace snatched up one of the flyers and sneered at it. "What makes you think anyone would want to set foot in that hole?"

Bess scrambled to her feet. Horace was smirking at her and to make matters worse she now saw Milly was with him. They both held striped paper bags and Bess guessed their parents had let them visit the sweetshop together. Her heart sank. Horace still hadn't forgiven her for the hook-a-wereduck incident and, since she'd been back at school, he and his friends had made a point of picking on Bess every chance they got.

Milly and the Unicorn Club had been as unpleasant as ever too. Bess tried to ignore them and desperately collected up the few remaining flyers before they could blow away.

"Look what a mess you've made," Horace went on in a loud voice. "I'm going to get Dad on to you for littering. What do you think, Milly?"

His sister nodded vigorously. "One of the ducks could eat a flyer and die."

Horace gave another smirk. "That's duck murder."

"I know you don't care about the ducks," Bess snapped. "I saw you kick one just yesterday. My pops always said you could tell a lot about a person by the way they treat animals."

"Your pops was a crackpot," Horace replied. "Just like you."

Bess felt a rising wave of anger in her chest. She knew that hitting people was wrong, but sometimes she really wanted to punch Horace right on his nose. She was about to say something very rude when she suddenly heard someone calling her name.

She turned to see Louie walking down the path, a huge smile lighting up his face.

Chapter 42

The Train of Dark Wonders had left once Bess was dropped off at home. She hadn't expected to see any of them again any time soon. Professor Ash had said he would leave a sack of magic beans at the Odditorium's station as soon as he could, but Bess hadn't heard anything from him yet.

Normally she would have been delighted at the sight of Louie in the rose garden, but she knew that he was exactly the sort of person Horace and Milly would take against. Louie was smartly dressed in a grey suit and he was gentle and softly spoken – all things that they would make fun of. Bess would just have to try to get him out of there as quickly as possible.

"I've got some good news!" Louie beamed, stopping beside her on the path. "But it can wait – I see you're in the middle of something with your friends."

"Don't call me her friend!" Horace couldn't have looked more disgusted.

Milly wore the same expression. "I'd never be friends with a freak like her."

But we were *friends!* Bess wanted to shout. *Once...* She still didn't understand what exactly had changed or how Milly could pretend they'd never been friends at all. It still hurt even now.

Louie's smile faded as he looked from Horace to Milly and back. "Oh. I see. Well, that's your loss. And don't call her a freak."

Bess took Louie by the arm. "Let's go," she muttered.

They started to walk away down the path and Bess desperately hoped Horace and Milly would let them leave without any further unpleasantness.

"I was trying to promote the Odditorium," she said quietly to Louie. "It's reopening tomorrow. But people aren't interested and now Horace has ruined my flyers."

It was hard not to feel frustrated. Bess had put so much effort into the Grand Reopening, but what was the point if people weren't even going to give the Odditorium a chance? Louie glanced around at the crowds milling about.

"How about a demonstration?" he whispered.

Bess glanced at him. "What kind of demonstration?"

"Hey!" Horace's voice rang out behind them. "I didn't say you could go. Either of you." He quickly caught them up, Milly at his heels, and shook a flyer in Bess's face. "I'll be there for your Grand Reopening tomorrow. And your pops won't be around to throw me out this time."

"I expect Bess will throw you out herself," Louie said. "But, if she's too busy seeing to more important things, then I'd be very happy to."

He reached into his jacket pocket and drew out the ghostly gobstopper.

Horace let out a bellow of a laugh. "*You?* You're skinny as a rake!"

"Oh yes, I'm much smaller than you," Louie agreed. He gave one of his mild smiles. "But I'm also a werewolf."

"You must think we're both stupid," Milly sneered.

"I hardly know either of you, but it does seem that way," Louie agreed. Then he popped the gobstopper into his mouth.

Horace lunged forward, but before he could lay a hand on Louie, there was a ripping, tearing sound as Louie's body transformed and his clothes fell away to reveal a snarling white wolf. Bess had forgotten how fearsome he looked up close. A line of drool hung down from his jaw and the fur on the back of his shoulders bristled. He really seemed like he would leap in for the attack at any moment.

Horace and Milly gave him one horrified look, then turned and fled, stumbling over their feet in their eagerness to get away. And the commotion hadn't been lost on the crowds of people in the rose garden either. All around, people were turning to stare, point and exclaim in horrified fascination at the sight of Bess Harper standing alone with a huge wolf. To complete the picture, Jet swooped down just then to settle on her shoulder in a flurry of black feathers.

Louie had stopped growling now that Horace and Milly had gone and he gave Bess a little nudge with his snout. She realised he wanted her to carry on walking down the path so she scooped up his clothes and then they set off together. They walked right out of the rose garden, past all the staring faces and up the front steps of the Odditorium. When Bess glanced over her shoulder, she saw that a whole crowd of people had followed her and were staring up at the museum.

"Grand Reopening tomorrow!" she called.

"Will the werewolf be there?" someone shouted.

"Come and find out," Bess replied.

Then she and Louie slipped into the museum and Bess locked the doors behind them. She showed Louie to her grandfather's old study and tossed in his clothes so he could turn back into a boy. He emerged from the room a few minutes later, smoothing back his hair.

Bess raised her eyebrows at him. "I thought you told Beau you weren't going to use your power to scare people."

He shrugged. "Well, I decided to make an exception. And anyway I don't think most of those people were *too* scared."

He was right. Bess guessed there was a difference between coming across a werewolf all alone in a forest in the middle of the night and seeing one in broad daylight in a rose garden. Besides, Louie hadn't been on the rampage or trying to attack anyone. A real-life werewolf was definitely a much better advert for the Odditorium then a flyer could ever be.

"Thanks," Bess said. "I owe you one."

"You definitely don't. Not after everything you did in the Land of Halloween Sweets." Louie grinned. "Actually that's why I'm here." He glanced at the raven still perched on Bess's shoulder. "Hello, Jet."

The raven inclined his head. "Thank you for acknowledging me. I was starting to think I'd turned invisible."

Bess rolled her eyes. "Don't mind him," she said. "He's ever so cranky."

"Well, perhaps this will cheer him up."

Louie reached into his pocket and pulled out a train ticket. It was similar to the one Professor Ash had given Bess before, only this one was gold rather than black.

"What's that?" she asked.

"It's a ticket for the Train of Dark Wonders," Louie said. "The ultimate ticket. It lets you come aboard whenever you want. We've only ever given one of these out once before."

"To Pops?" Bess said, staring at it in wonder.

"That's right. Dad had to get one specially made. That's why it's taken so long." He looked round the Odditorium. "I know this is your home and there are things you need to do here and you've got school and everything. But...well, schools have holidays, don't they? And you know what people are like when it comes to wonders. They always want something new and different and more exciting. So perhaps you might want to take another trip with us on the train sometime? Perhaps this doesn't have to be goodbye after all."

Bess's hand closed round the ticket and a huge smile spread over her face. "I can't think of anything I'd like more."

Jet seemed pleased by the prospect too. "Roseville bores me stiff," he complained. "I don't know how you've managed to live in this town for so long, Elizabeth. Nothing but roses and not so much as a cursed spinning wheel in sight."

With that, he swooped off to snaffle some sugared plums from a nearby dish.

"The train is parked up at Roseville's underground station right now," Louie went on. "Some of the gang wanted to have a picnic in the forest. We'll be there for another hour or so before we move on, so you could come and say hello to everyone if you like?"

Bess would have loved to join them, but she still had too much to do to get ready for the Odditorium's Grand Reopening. So she said a reluctant goodbye to Louie and returned to her final inspections. The feel of the train ticket in her pocket was a constant reminder that her adventures weren't over yet and Bess walked around with a permanent grin on her face.

At last, she was finished and walked back to Pops's study – or *her* study now, she supposed – to fetch her coat. But when she opened the door she found that the room was full of whispering flowers. They covered the walls and the ceiling, the desk and the bookshelves. Bess groaned aloud.

"Not this again! You can't possibly be hungry – you had loads of candy beetles recently!"

At least they hadn't broken anything this time, not even the window. Bess saw that they'd squeezed inside through the gap at the bottom of the door and that they'd been careful to avoid touching anything breakable. And there was something else that was different too. Normally the flowers all whispered different secrets, creating a murmuring hush of sound in which it was impossible to make out any individual words. But now they were all saying the same thing at the same time – the same two words repeated over and over again:

"*Elizabeth Harper, Elizabeth Harper, Elizabeth Harper.*"

Bess was startled. She'd never heard the flowers whisper her name before. She hadn't realised that they even knew what it was. It was odd to hear them all speaking together like that too. For the first time, she could make out the gravelly, whispery tone of their voice – strange and soft, like hearing a shadow speak. She took a step further into the room.

"I'm Elizabeth Harper," she said slowly. "And I'm listening."

"*We have a secret to share with you, Elizabeth. We know you come from a different world. One with spinning wheels, poisoned apples and crowns made of thorns. Henry Harper took something from that world – something that didn't belong to him.*"

That didn't sound right. Bess knew that Pops had had a strong moral code. He'd always paid a fair price for everything he'd collected and would never have taken an item against its owner's will. Perhaps there had simply been a misunderstanding.

"What do you think he took?" she asked.

"*One of Cinderella's magic slippers.*"

Something seemed to ripple through the air at the mention of Cinderella's name. Something cold and dark and dangerous. Bess gave a shiver and felt the hairs on her arms standing up.

The flowers rustled their leaves in an agitated sort of way. "*It's here,*" they went on, "*in the Odditorium.*"

"No, it isn't," Bess protested. "I've never seen anything like that, not even when I was cataloguing the exhibits."

"*There are corridors and chambers in this house that you know nothing of, Elizabeth Harper. Things your pops never showed you or wanted you to see. But heed our warning – Queen Cinderella is looking for that slipper. One day she's going to work out where it is. And she's going to want it back. Then we'll all be in danger. You'll see...*"

Acknowledgements

Many thanks to the following wonderful people:

My agent, Thérèse Coen, and all the people at the Hardman and Swainson Literary Agency and Susanna Lea Associates.

My editor, Katie Jennings. We've worked on many books together now and it's such a pleasure every time. You always make my story the best it can be – thank you, thank you.

Jane Tait – for her eagle-eyed, thoughtful and attentive copyedit. Helen Szirtes – for proofreading. And Beatriz Castro – for her brilliant, spooky cover and gorgeous internal artwork.

The rest of the team at Rock the Boat and Oneworld, including Paul Nash, Laura McFarlane, Ben Summers, Hayley Warnham, Mark Rusher, Lucy Cooper, Mary

Hawkins, Beth Marshall Brown, Deontaye Osazuwa, Matilda Warner, Julian Ball and Francesca Dawes.

My family.

All of the children's booksellers and teachers who take the time to champion books and nurture a love of reading in young people.

And, finally, to all of the children who have read and enjoyed my books. When you dress up as the characters, or write letters to me, or create things in the classroom, or share your amazing ideas at events, you remind me of what a special thing it is to be a children's writer. I hope you enjoy this book too.

ALEX BELL has written multiple books for both adults and young people, including *Frozen Charlotte*, a Zoella Book Club pick, and *The Polar Bear Explorers' Club*. After training as a lawyer, she now works at the Citizens' Advice Bureau. Alex lives in Hampshire with her husband, sons and demanding cats.